# Sunday Swap

# Books by Shalonda McFarland

## Non-Fiction
*A Christian's Worst Witness…From Being Broke to Being Blessed*
*A Christian's Worst Witness Workbook*
*Marriage Maintenance Workbook*

## Fiction
*The Win*
*The Win 2*
*Sunday Swap*

## Gag Books:
*The Perfect Pastor*
*The Perfect Church*

Sign up for my newsletter at ShalondaMcFarland.com to get notified of Pre-Orders (the lowest price available to reward my loyal supporters), Bonus Content, Freebies, etc.

# Sunday Swap

## Shalonda McFarland

Purpose Praise Publishing, Houston, TX

# Sunday Swap
## by Shalonda McFarland

Purpose Praise Publishing
P.O. Box 62425
Houston, TX 77205 U.S.A.

Verses marked KJV are taken from the King James Version of the Bible, Public Domain. All other versions used by permission from Zondervan via Biblegateway.com

Author Photo by Paula Boykin, Jones Photo Creations

McFarland, Shalonda
Sunday Swap / Shalonda McFarland

Paperback ISBN: 978-0-9885651-7-3

Library of Congress Control Number: 2020912094

1. Fiction 2. Religious 3. Fantasy

**Printed in the United States of America**

# 1 Nicole

MY ALARM CLOCK is blaring again. My covers feel like they weigh fifty pounds. There's no way it's six thirty already. I let out a sigh and debate whether to hit snooze a third time. Well, I already don't have time for breakfast, so I'd better get up and get going. Why are Mondays the hardest day to get up? I peel myself away from my pillow-top mattress bed and jump into action. I don't have much time to spare. I'm in and out of the bathroom in less than twenty minutes. I go to my walk-in closet and pick out an outfit from the five I ironed on Saturday and top it off with Mandy, my short-styled wig. I quickly choose my earrings and matching necklace out of my armoire then snatch my watch from the dresser and return to the bathroom for make-up. After applying my foundation, I peak at my watch. "Oh, I'll have to finish in the car." I grab my make-up bag and stuff it in my purse, get my laptop bag, and charge to the kitchen to retrieve a banana and a bottle of water.

My thirty to forty-minute ride into work hit the usual slow down spots and I'm able to finish my make-up waiting at the long stoplights, including penciling in my thin eyebrows and adding liner to my full lips. I pull up into the parking lot and turn the car off right at seven fifty-five and wash my banana down with water. After applying my lipstick, I grab my things and hurry to the front door.

I get to my floor and walk past the row of interview rooms, one of the doors is closed which means a recruiter is already conducting a candidate screening or interview. I remember those days, going through my inbox scanning for candidates, and revisiting files looking for the perfect match for an open position. Being a headhunter, as the industry calls it, is not for the faint at heart, if not for the fast pace, the hours can be long, and especially having your paycheck be eighty percent commission based. I'm a go getter though, which is how I've worked my way up to be an Account Executive which means I no longer deal with the potential candidates who are looking for a job, but the companies who want to hire our agency to supply them with candidates, a work force of either temporary, contract, or permanent employees.

"WorkReady Staffing Agency how may I help you?" I hear the receptionist say in the background. The office is awakening with calls; one person is walking an applicant through what they will expect when they take a personality test at a job site, another is asking a job-seeker if they are willing to relocate to a small town, and another is trying to pinpoint what his candidate's salary walkaway point is so he'll know when to let a potential job go as he conducts negotiations. I smile and walk into my office.

"You really put that outfit together. I never catch you slipping."

I turn around. "Thanks Jenny."

"You always dress to a T."

I look down at my purple blouse and belted A-line skirt and shrug my shoulders. "It matches the buckles of my heels."

"And your purse. You sure you don't do a fashion blog on the side?"

I laugh. "No, not at all. My plate is full enough already."

"Like I've told you before, if you ever have a garage sale or give your clothes to Goodwill, please keep me in mind."

Although Jenny is a little taller than I am, she could probably fit my clothes if she altered them to be about two inches smaller, especially in the derriére. I shake my head and turn on my computer to get started. Our meeting starts in less than an hour and I want to look at a few things before I head over.

I step into the conference room and join the usual crew. I immediately notice Jenny at the coffee pot, not because she's the only one walking around, but because her dark red hair can't help but be noticed. I sit and wait with the others for our manager to start the meeting. Gary rolls in a little after nine, apologizing because he had just gotten off a conference call with his boss. He goes over some industry news, corporate initiatives, and shares where we are against our target numbers and gives us our marching orders for the week. He also announces that he's picked me to work on the proposal for a big potential client. This is a great way to start the week. I've been wanting to increase my client base and if I land this client, it will directly impact my career. So far, my clients have been in the three to eight-million-dollar range, but this new client, a software developer with offices downtown, will generate twenty-five million annually for the company. I can't wait to get started on our proposal.

# 2 Darnell

I'M ALREADY AWAKE. I look over at the clock which shows 5:15 am. God must have me up for a reason, so I get out of bed and start praying fifteen minutes earlier than normal. I go through my normal sequence of Adoration, Confession, Thanksgiving, and Supplication and add my mental list of prayer targets, for the world, our country and local government, for God to bless his people with emotional, financial, and spiritual health and give me continued wisdom to lead the church he's placed me in. I add a family who has been heavy on my heart. When I finish, the clock shows 6:30, so I turn on the radio and listen to Gospel music as I wash up and get dressed. Even though I'm not in nearly the shape I was in during my basketball days in college, you can't tell by my physique. I've still got the same slim frame, I just can't run a mile without stopping, or more realistically, not even while jogging.

I go for my morning run, eat a bowl of oatmeal, and return to my already-open Bibles and commentaries and continue my study. Before I know it, it is eleven o'clock and almost time for lunch. I turn on the television and watch thirty minutes of the news, eat, and switch gears to work on Sunday's sermon and sketch out Wednesday's bible study. I look at my calendar for the week and notice I have three hospital visits and an appointment with the plumber to see why the sink and dishwasher at the church are not working correctly. I also need to look over the church's yearly, quarterly, and monthly budget and see where we are versus projections and look over the goals and budget submissions for each ministry before the leadership meeting.

My phone rings. My watch shows 6:45pm. I put my head in my hands. It's a call from one of my members, panicked about a physical altercation she had with her husband. They both want me to come over to their house and help them solve the disagreement. They say it was either me or the cops. I tell them I'll be right over. This isn't the first interruption of the day, but it may prove to be the biggest. I put my pen inside my notebook and close it. *I'll have to finish this whenever I get back,* I conclude. I pick up my bible and keys and head out to do ministry.

# 3 Nicole

I GLANCE AT my watch. It's already 5:45pm. The day has sped by me. I stand on my tippy toes in order to peek over the tops of the cubicles to see if anyone else is here. I sigh. The only one I see is the cleaning guy emptying everyone's trash cans. I need to wrap up this document and get going so I can make it to church on time. I'm also hungry. I'm glad I didn't go out to eat today because I would have finished working much later than this but the sandwich I packed didn't hold me. I also need to stop and get something for everyone to eat for tonight's meeting. I'll call in a to-go pizza order. I'll have to eat my slices along the way because I'll be too busy taking notes during the meeting. *Oh, I've got to go to the bathroom before I leave here, that's a long way, and traffic still won't have died down yet.*

I get back from the bathroom and gather my things, then lock my office door as I walk out. I glance at the wall clock and the time of 6:05 is practically screaming at me, sounding the alarm that I am late, late, late. Pastor will not be happy at all. I'll have to make up the time behind the wheel. *Lord, please don't let me get a ticket.*

I call when I get close to the church to have one of the brothers help get the food out of my car. After I make it to the fellowship hall and sit down, I glance at my watch, 7:08. Not bad if I say so myself. *Thank you, Lord, for getting me here in one piece.* They haven't even started the meeting yet. Brother Larkin blesses the food and as soon as everyone gets their slices and sits down, pastor officially starts the meeting.

We go over each ministry leader's submitted goals and calendar for the year as Pastor asks them questions and refines what their goals should be, confirms who's on their team, as well as adjusts their budgets. I have the master church calendar already on the screen with all the individually requested ministry dates pastor had given me earlier this week included, so everyone can see from a big picture, what's happening each month.

Here is where he goes on his rant, questioning how much thought some leaders have put into this whole process, making many ministries streamline their events into one or two each that really impact the body as a whole. He also asks the leaders to give a deeper thought as to whether the event lines up with each particular ministry's purpose. This adds another fifteen minutes to the meeting. He should have called and talked to those leaders personally if he felt they needed to change something. Why should we all have to hear this? Let me put my pen down, maybe he'll catch the hint. Who call's a meeting on a Friday night anyway? There're a hundred other things I can be doing right now. Now Tina's asking a specific question about her ministry. We don't need to hear this. She needs to set up a one on one appointment with Pastor because her problem doesn't pertain to us. What can I do to pass the time? If I check my phone, I'll look unprofessional. Portia, one of the leaders, is staring at my hand. Oh, it's because I'm clicking my nails on the table. *Stop it.* I deliberately lay my hand flat to remind myself to be still. I glance around the room to make sure no one else notices. A few look at me as if they want me to save them. I raise my eyebrows and purse my lips as if to say *look, I didn't call this meeting.* I look down and notice I need a refill. I need to remember to call and make a nail appointment. I think I'll change the color from hot pink to green. *Why not?*

"Nicole?"

Oh, how long has he been calling my name? "Uh, yes?"

"Set Tina up an appointment with me so we can discuss this further."

"My pleasure." It's about time. Now we can move on to something else.

After going through each line item on the pastor's agenda, including having the deacons change a few things around communion, we officially adjourn the meeting at 8:45pm. This is not the relaxing Friday night I was hoping for. As soon as pastor says Amen, we all, me included, scatter so fast you'd think we have smelt someone passing gas.

# 4 Nicole

MY WEEKEND WAS a blur. By the time I arrived home after the meeting Friday night, and took a shower, I was too tired to do anything else. I fell asleep watching CNN. Saturday, I was so busy cleaning up and getting prepared for the week, I didn't even have time to turn the television on.

After the church body sings the benediction song, *Lord be with you, Lord be with you, Lord be with you until we meet again,* I look at my watch to see what time the meeting will start. Pastor didn't give a specific time, he just said meet at his house thirty minutes after church is over. What he really means is thirty minutes after he leaves the church, because it may take him that long just to greet those who want to shake his hand or tell him how nice the message was.

I say hello to a few people then grab my things and leave. I drive to the next couple of stops I need to make. I could be at home relaxing right now. Before I know it, it will be time to get ready for work. Time seems to disappear on Sunday's. He has no idea how much my time is worth. If I got paid at church, even half of what my salary is on the job, he'd take me more seriously. I'm qualified to do more than just write the minutes at these financial meetings, well any meeting for that matter. He trusts me enough to give me his house key but not enough to listen to what I have to say about important matters regarding the church. Or he may have just bestowed me his key for convenience. After all, I'm his errand girl. Huh, that's exactly what this is. I'm not privileged; it's just easier for him to have me pick up everything so he doesn't have to do it himself. I throw the box of chicken and rolls down on the counter and let the bag with the containers of red beans and rice slip from my grasp. "Huh, if that would have fallen over, it would've stayed right there. I wasn't going to pick it up. I've done enough. Let me go ahead and eat," I tell the empty house.

The doorbell keeps ringing each time someone new shows up. It's only customary though, they all know it's unlocked, and I've got everything ready as usual. All they have to do is come in and sit down.

"Have you started already?" Pastor Thompson playfully asks when he finally shows up.

"Pastor, you know the meeting doesn't officially begin until you sit down." Trustee Larkin says, peaking over his glasses.

Here's my cue. I take out my yellow note pad and pen.

"Sister Freeman, are you gonna eat?"

"I already did."

"You didn't wait on the brothers?" he smiles. "We can all eat and talk through the topics until we get down to the financial part. That's really when you'll need to write."

We need to get this show on the road, I don't plan on being here all day. "I write down everything and I can't very well eat with a pen and paper in my hand, unless you want chicken grease on your notes."

"OK Sister, OK."

We talk for about half an hour, first recapping today's service. It was a great service. Pastor's message was anointed as usual, and so compelling. We had five people join church, and two gave their lives to Christ. When we move on to heavier matters, I just have to say something. "I'm concerned about the lighting you're proposing to get installed. I don't think this whole lighting system is right for our church."

"What is that based on?" Pastor asks.

"What is the purpose of the spotlights? And look at the cost of it."

"Nicole, our church is going through a transition. We need to attract the younger crowd that are avoiding going to church. This generation is not finding the church."

"But Pastor, you think lights is the answer? Won't it alienate faithful church members that are not looking for that?"

"There are many churches that have renovated their sanctuaries; taking out pews and replacing them with stackable chairs and getting rid of the choir stand and going to more of a praise and worship team. And these churches still survived, they're actually thriving."

"Can't the money be better spent somewhere else though? I think you're taking us too far, too fast."

"We don't want to get stagnant, we want to be viable now. I want our church to have a contemporary feel not necessarily traditional."

"But we have a traditional church. I agreed with getting rid of devotion but getting rid of the choir for a praise team is a big adjustment for any church, young or old." I express.

"Why did you agree with getting rid of devotion? That's part of the foundation of the church itself?" Bro. Larkin asks.

"We still have a minister read a scripture and pray; they just don't take thirty minutes doing it," I say.

"That's what's wrong with these young folks today. They say it don't take all that, but that's exactly what got us through."

"Brother Larkin, no disrespect but the prayers were getting to be mundane and very long. A public devotion is not the time to be long-winded. When you're praying like you're supposed to at home, you don't feel the need to pray long drawn-out prayers in public. Some of the deacons are trying to make up for what they don't do in private and pass it off in public like it's something they do all the time. I can see right through that," Pastor says.

"Well, that's one thing we agree on." I point to pastor then address everyone. "I mean, I appreciate the Lord not letting my bed be my cooling board, but do I have to hear that every Sunday?"

"Well I'll say," Brother Larkin shakes his head.

"Pastor, at least with the choir, we had some type of pattern. We knew we'd have two songs and a song during the invitation. With the praise team, they sing four or five songs before you get up to preach. That's a bit much. They're having a mini concert every Sunday," I say.

"Nicole, it's okay to try something new." Pastor then looks around the table. "Our church is still built on the Word, we're just changing with the times," he adds.

"But I don't know how I feel having church service in the dark with different color lights beaming and shining spotlights. It's just not us. When I get up on Sunday morning I want to go to church, not to a concert." I want to tell him they have the same lights at the strip club, or so I'm told, but I don't want to push it too far. I might give Brother Larkin a heart attack. "That's what the shining lights feel like...a concert, an attraction, not the house of worship. It feels like a gimmick."

"I understand perfectly Sister Freeman. I get it, but I'm going to do something different. That's the direction that I feel like we need to go in."

I look around the table for some support from the other brothers but all I get is silence. Deacon Joe raises his eyebrows and wrinkles his mouth as if he's telling me he's sorry I got shot down. The others are avoiding eye contact, one looking at his shirt, the other shaking his head, apparently OK with everything Pastor has lined out. I don't know how the ones who aren't here, feel about all the changes. Between prior engagements, a few who work this Sunday, and vacations, only a few deacons are even here. Maybe they've already voiced their opinions to the pastor but got shot down. Who knows?

I try another angle to see if he'll just say 'no' without really figuring out what my grievance is about. "Pastor, I don't think you're taking into consideration the youth leaders' vacation bible school budget."

"No, I've thought about all that."

I lean back in my chair.

"I appreciate the fact that you don't just agree with me, but actually state your convictions, even if we disagree, which we normally do."

Those words give me no comfort. I continue to take notes but don't say much of anything else the rest of the meeting.

Trustee Larkin, Deacon Joe, and Brother Gladwell are all older men, at least in their sixties. I'm surprised this doesn't bother them. I'm the youngest. If anything, I should know what I, as well as the younger crowd, would enjoy when it comes to the ambience of our church. And Pastor may rethink this when he's in the middle of his sermon and see many of the older people in the congregation asleep under the dark lighting.

The meeting's over and everyone's leaving but I still need to talk to him. Maybe he's more willing to really listen without the brothers here. Maybe he thought he needed to prove something to them by shutting me down. After the last person leaves, I push the chairs up to the table and stand behind one of them.

"Pastor, there were a couple of topics we discussed today that I don't think you're really considering all the consequences if we do it the way you've laid out."

"Don't you think the Lord would tell me first, on any decision concerning the church?"

"Maybe He has but you aren't listening."

Well that gets his attention. He lowers his papers and looks me in the eye.

"No disrespect Pastor, but if all you needed was God's voice, why would you even need leaders in the church? You can learn from the people in the congregation too, you know."

He's not saying anything, so I keep talking. "God used Jethro to show Moses a better way, so He doesn't always have to tell you directly. I've been here for years. I've seen the effects of change and you have to be careful. You're just coming in. Granted, you've made an impact in these last few months, but you should listen more to what your people are saying. You can't just force change down their throats, you've got to get their buy in, their support."

"Nicole."

I don't take a breath. "Don't just tell them what they're gonna do; ask them if they think it's the right thing *to* do. I really hope you reconsider. Have a good day, Pastor."

I grab my purse off the floor and stuff my notepad inside. I'm leaving. He can clean this mess up by himself.

***

When I finally do get home, it's after 4pm and after my phone conversations with my mom and sister, I watch a couple of detective shows, then a game show, and now I'm ready to wind down. I start thinking about the meeting this afternoon. Pastor means well but he doesn't seem too keen to take advice from others. He's different than Pastor Andrews in a lot of ways, not that I expected him to be like Pastor Andrews but at least my late pastor was more approachable. I don't like the friction between me and Pastor Thompson. I hope he's making the right decisions.

I doze off a couple times lying in bed with my reading glasses on. I sigh, tilt my Bible down, pull off my glasses and mutter, "Even Moses was wise enough to take Jethro's advice." *Lord, make him see what I see. If he could just step into my shoes, he'd understand.* "Lord, do what only you can do, and open his eyes." I turn the nightstand light off and fall into sleep.

(Seconds later, a soft wind seeps through the window.)

# 5 Darnell

I'M SITTING IN my chair in the living room reflecting on the meeting and replaying in my mind the altercation with Nicole. I know she was upset with me by the way she quickly left. She normally stays and helps clean up, but that's fine. I managed. I've only been at this church a short time and I need to make sure I set standards, so people won't think they can walk all over me. It's better to loosen up than to have to tighten up, so I need to stick to what I've committed to. I am the pastor and after everything is said and done, it all falls back on me, whatever decision I make. I've just got to keep praying so I can hear from God and make the best decision for everyone involved. *Lord, maybe I was hard on her. Am I hearing you, Lord? She just doesn't understand all the things I have to consider. She should be in my shoes.* "Huh, she wouldn't last a day." Just the thought makes me laugh. I get out of my chair, turn the lights off and go to my room to get ready for bed. "Lord, do what only you can do."

(Seconds later, an undetectable breeze enters through the closed window.)

# 6 Nicole

WOW, WHY AM I woke? It's still pitch-black outside. I look over at the clock on the nightstand. *5 am. No, Lord. You know I don't do mornings.* I still have another hour and a half before I must get up. I wasn't feeling well last night anyway. After I laid down and closed my eyes, I had trouble sleeping. I felt restless, which is unusual for me. It doesn't even feel like I've been sleeping for very long. Monday morning sure comes early. I surrender to my drowsiness and allow myself to go back to sleep.

My eyes reopen. It's not quite pitch dark but it is still hard to see. I glance at the clock again. An hour and a half has passed. "Well, this is my normal time. I wonder why the clock didn't alarm." I'm laying here gathering my thoughts of what I need to do for the day. "OK, I've just got to get donuts, the documents are already in— What the—" There's a big lump under the covers. "Oh my God, Jesus! Jesus!" There's something crawling on me. I jump out of bed and within three long strides make it far enough from the bed so whatever it is can crawl out. But I've got to pay attention to see what it is and where it's going. I need to turn on the light. I feel my way to the wall while keeping my eyes on the bed, my heart is pounding, anticipating what will surface from the covers. That better not be a mouse. I pay too much for this condo for them not to keep it clean. Let that be a mouse in here, and I promise I'm gonna go off. This is ridiculous.

Did I have too much to drink last night? I can't even find the light switch. Wait, I didn't even drink anything last night. I can't even see my room clear enough. The animal, where is it? It's not moving. I don't hear a thing. I need a stick or something. Jesus, I can't see. I frantically search down the wall until I find the switch. Before I can dart my eyes back to the bed I realize the creature isn't under the covers but in my shorts. I snatch them down and feel my eyes pop out of my head. I triple blink and feel myself falling to the floor. I can't control my body. I feel my eyes rolling backward.

# 7 Darnell

*AM I AWAKE? No, I'm dreaming.* These covers feel good, I'm not even hot. Let me scratch my chest. Very funny. Man, I feel like I'm rubbing a woman's breasts. *Lord, please don't let me have these kinds of dreams, you know I'm trying to stay right with you. Without thinking, my hand automatically finds its way into my shorts. No, don't give in, even in your sleep.* I force my hand out of my shorts and to my side. *You need to go back to sleep.*

\*\*\*

The sound of the alarm clock breaks through the dead silence and snatches me out of my rest. I look over at the clock on the nightstand and push whatever button I can find to stop the annoying invasion. "6:30? Why am I so tired? Lord, what did I do last night? Yesterday was a normal day of preaching." I reach down to adjust myself. I move my hand up and down, but I don't feel anything. *I'm lying on my package. Huh, that's a first.* I open my legs and lift.

I reach down to flip it back up and what the—I snatch the covers off, jump out of bed, and at the same time I pull down my shorts. I'm touching everywhere, searching my body in the front and back for my parts. I hear an ear-piercing scream. "Jesus!" That's exactly what I'm screaming, but that's not my voice. My heart. It's pounding in my ears. Am I having a heart attack? The light shining through the blinds guides me to the door where I yank the light switch. My head shoots down and I grab what...what is not there. My hand goes further, reaching behind because my piece has gone way south. I check behind both legs, so it's got to be stuck in between my butt cheeks. I reach back and...and, nothing. My chest heaves in and out. *Jesus, I haven't done weed since college. You forgave me for that, Lord. What is this? I'm trippin'.* I close my eyes and slip into darkness.

***

I'm coherent, I think. I'm looking at the ceiling. I raise up slowly but stay seated on the hardwood floor. I stand and take all my clothes off. I find the bathroom and splash water on my face and look in the mirror. This can't be happening. It's not even possible. I slap myself and blink. Nope, nothing's changed. And I'm certainly not dreaming. *Lord, what's happening?* My heart keeps pounding. Who am I? I look down and I see all woman parts. I cup the breasts. Yep, these are real. I turn around and look at my backside through the mirror. I am in a woman's body. I lean closer to the mirror. "Whose body is this?" I touch the face and look into the eyes. I know this person, but I can't make out who it is. I don't remember anyone who wears their hair like this. *Think. Look for clues.* I look at my hands. Bright pink nails, I've seen them somewhere, but I don't remember on who.

I look around the bedroom then open the door and walk into the living room. From here I see the kitchen, but no one is in the apartment but me. I turn, and something catches my eye. There on the kitchen table is our church mug, Abiding Grace, the words in gold. OK, it's got to be someone at my church. I go back into the bedroom and look for a purse. There it is on the dresser. I rummage through it to find a wallet. I undo the clasp and open it. Right there in front is the driver's license. Her picture tells me, but her name on the right confirms it. Line one: Freeman, line two: Nicole Amber. "Nicole!"

I pull open the drawers and search for some clothes to put on. I find a shirt and shorts and dart into the closet where I see some tennis shoes on the floor. I pull everything onto this body I'm in as quickly as I can and grab her purse, phone and keys. I look around the room again. I don't think I need anything else, so I lunge for the front door.

I look up and see the sign for the parking garage elevator. I get on and push the first button that says G5. When I emerge from the elevator, I'm on the top floor of the garage and I immediately push the red button on her key fob and listen. I don't hear anything, so I run down the ramp. *Oh, wow.* Pain stops me as I grab my chest. I forgot to put a bra on. I debate whether to go back to the room but decide to hold them in place instead. I'm running with one arm keeping these breasts from moving and the other clutching this purse. I keep running, level after level, until I hear the blaring alarm. I get into her car and call my cell phone again but it's no use. No one picks up. I activate the navigation system on her phone, input my address, and head to my house.

I pass by trees and cars like they're a blur. The tires screech as I turn the corner on my street. I'm glad rush hour is over, I'd probably have gotten pulled over by now. I pull up to my house. I don't know what I'm going to find. My truck's not in the driveway, I think I parked it in the garage last night. I pull hard into the driveway and almost forget to put it in park, I'm halfway out of the car before I remember to shut the car off and take the keys. I sprint to the porch and snatch the spare key from under the designated rock and unlock the front door. I barge in nearly running, then stop mid glide to go back and close the door. I lock it and slowly turn around, catching my breath. I don't hear anything. I make one glance over the kitchen and living room, and nothing is out of place. I carefully walk around. I feel like I'm prowling around someone else's home. I don't know what to expect. I go to my bedroom. My chest is heaving. I get to my closed door and don't know if I should knock, yank the door open, or slowly creep in. My mind is racing. I slowly raise this foreign hand and turn the knob, as I peak around the opening door.

I'm on the ground. I mean, my body is on the ground, laying there, lifeless. *Oh, God, no. Jesus, am I dead?* This can't be, there is no such thing as reincarnation. *It is appointed unto men once to die, but after this the judgment. Hebrews 9:27, I remind myself.* I rush to…me, my own body and put my head, well her head, to my chest, listening for any sound of life. *Oh, a heartbeat. Thank God. What is this Lord?* I start pacing the floor. *Why am I in her body? Absent from the body is present with the Lord. This makes no sense. And I never wanted to be a woman. Wait, so if I'm in her body, Oh Lord, she's got to be in mine. Think, think! OK OK, she probably fainted too.*

My body is cooler than normal, maybe because it's on this floor. I pull my own body to the wall and place it up against it. Maybe sitting my body up will wake her up. I grab a blanket and place it on my body too. Maybe I should call 911. I jolt to the phone on my nightstand. But I don't need anyone dispatched. *Think.* OK I can tell them it's a non-emergency, and tell them she fainted, I fainted, he—I've got to remember to say he. No, they'd still probably send someone over here. And when she wakes up I don't know how she's going to react. What will she say? They may think she's crazy, or on drugs. They may want to lock her up in a psych ward and pump my body up with real drugs. That's not happening. I slam the phone down. I rush to my body and slap it, hard. Harder. No movement. I open my own eye lid. Nothing. I slap my nonresponsive body again. Again. I sink down on the floor, not sure what else to do.

*Think.* Who can I call? If I call *my* pastor, he'll think I'm in looney-ville. He'll never look at me the same way. If I call one of my ministers they'll think me and Nicole have something going on and just had a crazy night. Wait, my dad. No, he'll think it's a joke, and so will my brother. I'll never hear the end of it. I have no one. I can't get anyone else involved in this. Who'll believe me anyway?

But, I've got to at least get my body woke. How do you recover someone who's fainted, or maybe hit their head? I take the cell phone out of my pocket and place it on the ground and start feeling my head for any big bumps. Oh, I'll ask Google. "Hey Goog—" Oh, I feel sick. I think I'm gonna throw up. I rush to the bathroom. I yank the door open so hard that it bounces back and closes behind me. I spew out whatever nervousness is inside me and hold on to the toilet bowl like it's my long-lost friend. I rinse my mouth out in the sink. I'm breathing long and deep. I lean against the wall and allow my body to slide down then I sit on the cold floor. I just need a minute to get myself together.

# 8 Nicole

I OPEN MY eyes. Ouch. Why does my face hurt? Why am I sleeping straight up on the floor? Oh, I had the craziest dream. Where in the world did that come from? And why am I so groggy? I'm looking around. "Why am I in the Pastor's house? Oh my, I fell asleep over his house? How? Well, at least he's a gentleman. He gave me my space." I look down and there's a blanket covering me. Well that's nice of him to cover me up but, how in the world am I going to explain this? This looks terrible. Me, sleeping over the pastor's house! How am I going to leave without anybody seeing me? He probably has nosey neighbors. I stand. I've got to find my purse. This is embarrassing. I've got to get out of here before he sees me. *Nicole, don't make a sound, and he won't hear me.* I dart around the room looking for my purse and--oh, there he is. I immediately fall to the ground. Oh my God, Oh my God, he's up. Shoot. This is silly, I can't avoid him. This is his house. Just say, 'Good Morning,' apologize and leave.

I breathe in and out a couple of times and say it. "Good morning." I hear his deep voice. Oh, he beat me to it. "Good morning, I a...pol...o...gize." Is he mocking me or are we just thinking the exact same thing? And why is he talking so loud, I can't even hear myself? "Look, I doooonn't knnnnooooow..." I slur my words because his voice seems to actually come from my mouth. I move closer to him. And he's moving toward me, our eyes are locked. "Pastor I— why does my voice sound like yours? Why are you mimicking me? He doesn't say anything back. I turn slightly to the left and then to the right. What in the world? I don't know why I do it, but I do...I shake my body. "Why are you mimicking me? Pastor Darnell, that's not funny. Why do I sound like you?" OK that's enough, this is creepy. I put my hands up and say "Stop" Wait, what the—? My hands, these aren't my—I look down at my body. I look up and charge toward him...my hand hits the...mirror! I keep touching the mirror, like I'm trying to find a way out. "What is this?" I keep my eyes straight ahead. I touch my face all over. I feel hair on my chin, under my lip, a mustache. I look down frantically touching myself. I SCREAM!

# 9 Darnell

A SCREAM AWAKENS me out of my stupor. I immediately open the bathroom door and bolt into the room, my bedroom. I see my body turn from the mirror and stare at me. I see my own eyes bulging. I gasp. The sight of me took the sound from her mouth. She's standing there horrified. Both of us speechless and winded, our chests moving in and out, trying to keep our hearts contained within their walls.

"What is this?"

"How can this be?"

We're talking over each other and nothing makes any sense. "Nicole, this is you right?" I open my hands for her to observe the body that I'm in. She shakes her head.

"Pastor!"

"Yeah, it's me."

"Wha—"

"I don't have a clue. This isn't possible."

"This can't be happening. This CAN'T happen!" Her voice escalates. "Why am I in your body?"

"I don't know." I start to rub my forehead. I don't know what to do. "Lord, what is this? This can't be real."

"What happened last night?" Nicole asks.

"Nothing. I don't know, I just remember going to sleep."

"Think." She told herself. "How did you get here?" she directs to me.

"I woke up in what must be your apartment. I didn't know it was you at first, so I looked through your purse and saw your driver's license in your wallet."

"What, what do you mean you didn't know it was me? Didn't you look in the mirror?"

I frown. "You look totally different without make-up and—" I wave my hand over her body's hair which is in multiple rows of plaits going straight back. "I've never seen you look like this."

She scrunches her face, my face, and I look…irritated.

"But why, what is this? Why did this happen? We need to think, retrace our steps. What exactly did you do up until you went to sleep? Because I was in my own bed before I went to sleep. Then I woke up here. So, whatever happened, happened while we were sleep."

We detail our day and night, including our frustration with each other during the meeting yesterday afternoon. Like her, I was still thinking

32

about it right before I went to bed. And like me, she said something to the Lord about being able to see things from her perspective.

"So, you prayed that God would let me know what it's like to be you…oh, come on, I know he answers preachers' prayers fast but please, give me a break."

"It wasn't a prayer, I just said it, as a joke."

"Does this look like a joke to you?"

"You said something similar yourself. Don't put it all on me."

"Well take it back. Come on Pastor, let's get on our knees. And you pray."

She pulls me down to the floor. We're at the edge of the bed and she nods me to start. I pray for a long time. I decree and declare it be so. I open my eyes. Nothing happens.

"Maybe I need to do it, since I'm in your body," she tells me.

She prays and claims it in Jesus' name. Nothing changes.

"Maybe we should be holding hands, you know touching and agreeing," she says.

It makes sense. We do that. We both pray out loud, together. I slowly open my eyes. "Are you praying in faith?"

"Yes! Are you in faith?" she snaps back.

"Of course."

"Then what's the problem? Is God punishing you for something? What did you do?"

"I didn't do anything. And why can't it be you? I know my lifestyle, I'm a pastor, but I don't know about *yours*."

"I haven't done anything."

This blaming back and forth is pointless. We sit in silence, out of ideas. She jolts up. "I'm late for work. I need to call in." She reaches for her phone and dials a number. "Hey Janice, I'm not coming in today, I'm really sick…It's Nicole. Well, yeah, that's how sick I am, I sound like a man. Tell Gary for me. OK, thanks. I will."

She looks at me. "Well, until we can figure out how to switch this back. We need to get a game plan together."

"What do you want to do?"

She sits back, putting distance between us. "First, you need to brush your teeth. What in the world!"

"Right, long story."

***

We decide to both go stay in her condo since it's less vulnerable to nosey neighbors or passersby, and so we can drive Nicole's car back to her place. I pick up a few essentials, including clothes, my toothbrush, phone and charger, and my Bible. I turn everything off in the house and lock up.

Nicole abruptly stops when she sees her car jaggedly parked. "I see you must have been really scared."

I shrug my shoulders. There's no need to deny it. I walk around the car and without thinking, I get in on the passenger's side and she the driver's side.

"Oh!" Nicole shouts.

"That sounded painful. What was that?"

"I hit my head on the door frame."

"Oh, right."

I'm already in my seat but she's trying to maneuver my six-foot body into the car. She adjusts her seat to take her knees away from the steering wheel and lowers the chair, so her head isn't too high.

"I'm not used to your body," she states the obvious.

"I see."

"Do you want to drive?"

"I don't know the way."

"Then how did you get here?"

"The GPS on your phone."

"How did you get my phone open? You don't know my password."

"Your fingerprint."

"Right." She shakes her head. "Why didn't you call me when you first discovered…this?" She gestures to both of us.

"I did, but I forgot I put my phone on silent before I go to bed."

"Why would you do that?

"Because sometimes I don't want to be bothered."

She raises an eyebrow. "What about your house phone?"

"I put that on silent too."

"Whatever works for you." She shrugs her shoulders, my shoulders, and puts the car in reverse.

"Wait, what if someone sees who they think is me, driving your car? Doesn't that look bad?"

"If they look that hard and can see through these tinted windows, more power to 'em."

The drive back to her place is surreal. I pinch myself pretty good just to make sure I'm not in some sort of elaborate dream. We make the trek in about thirty minutes. This morning it felt like I drove it in fifteen. I know I should have gotten pulled over, but I thank God for the small things.

We pass the marquee that brandishes the name La Chateau Condominiums and pull into the five-story parking garage. The lift-gate opens automatically from the sensor decal on her windshield.

We drive up two levels before we see an open spot where she stops and parks.

"Hey, how did you find my car, anyway?"

"I started at the fifth floor, pushed the car alarm and ran down until I heard it."

"I know you ran down at least three levels!"

"I was running on adrenaline, straight adrenaline."

We make our way to the eighth floor and turn left coming out of the elevator. The hallways are bordered with dark gray carpet that coordinate with the lighter gray walls. The sea of stone-gray doors stand at attention like British soldiers. There are red fixtures on the ceiling that hold the main lights and small lamps that hang on each side of the wall between every second door. The lampshades allow light to shine from the top and bottom, cascading the wall like headlight beams.

We get into Nicole's apartment, well condo, and she slowly walks around.

"This feels weird. It's like I'm looking at everything from a different angle," she says.

"I know what you mean. It's about a five-inch adjustment. It doesn't sound like much, but it makes a big difference."

"So what, we just wait this thing out until tomorrow?"

"Yeah, sounds good to me."

"OK, Well my computer's over there. I can try and get some work done. Why don't we get something to eat?"

"I think I'm going to fast tonight, study, and pray that this thing reverse itself tomorrow. Let's make sure we pray together right before we go to sleep."

"Yeah, OK. That's a good idea."

"Where do you want me to sleep?"

"You can sleep in my bed, maybe being closer will reverse this thing."

"Good thinking. I'll try anything at this point."

When it's time to go to bed, we don't just get down on our knees, we lay prostrate on the floor, the lowest physical posture I know. We want to show our complete surrender to Him and pray this thing reverse itself. That's the only thing we can do; pray.

# 10 Nicole

THE ALARM CLOCK goes off. Acting on autopilot, I quickly turn it off and lay there. I'm gathering my thoughts. What am I feeling? Am I dreaming? Was this an elaborate, insane dream? My memories of yesterday catch up to me. I close my eyes and move my hand over my chest...nothing. I slide my hand under the covers and under my clothes...yep something. I shoot straight up. I see me, well my body, sitting on the couch by the wall. I watch my body look at me and shake its head.

"No, not again," I say, snatching the covers off. "Why? Why is this happening to us? How long is this going to be like this? I have a life." I know these are questions Darnell can't answer but I ask them anyway. "I can only be sick for a couple days without having a doctor's note."

"Huh, don't think for a second that I'm going into work for you."

"You got a better idea?"

"You'll need to ask for a vacation or a leave of absence."

"I can't, I just received a big project, something that I've been asking for, for a long time. And I finally got it. It's an opportunity to show what I can do. I can't mess this up. They'll think I'm cracking under the pressure. My boss will think he made a mistake giving me this shot. There's no way I can take vacation, not until I get this done. And I've never called in sick before. And what do you plan on doing with the church?"

"I can have someone fill in for me for a while. We can wait this out. There's no need for you to go up there."

"I'm fine with that. Listen, since we're going to be each other. Oh Lord, for I don't know how long. We've got to learn each other's body."

He shakes his head in agreement.

"Right now, I've got to use the bathroom. I did it yesterday, but I don't know if I did it right." I walk quickly to my bathroom.

"Huh, your job's much easier than mine. "How have you been doing it?" Darnell doesn't try to hide the sarcasm.

"I sat on the toilet, I guess out of habit, but I've always wanted to be able to pee standing up. So how do I do this?"

"Easy. You just point and shoot."

"But how do I keep my pants from falling down?"

"Your butt will hold them up."

I do what he says and immediately liquid splashes on the seat.

He quickly grabs. "You've got to hold it."

He lets go after I take the reins. I finish and reach for some toilet tissue.

"What are you gonna do with that?"

"Wipe the pee off my...*your* thing."

"Nuh uh, shake two times and put it back in there."

"Ughh that's gross." I comply then take the tissue and wipe the seat. "Come on, you need to go too so we don't have to come back in here."

"I can do this." He sits down and when he finishes, at least he does get the toilet tissue.

"Stop. No." I know my eyes are bigger than Dallas. "You can't do it like that, you're gonna give me a bladder infection! Front to back, always wipe front to back. Lord, have mercy."

"I can't even see it with all this—"

"Good. You don't need to. And that's none of your business."

I reach for the soap. "And you make sure you wash *your* hands." I'm shaking my head. *Lord, give me strength.* This is going to be a trip.

# 11 Darnell

It's now Wednesday, and we woke up this morning still in each other's bodies after another day of praying and searching the scriptures. We prayed together at least three times yesterday. While I was studying, she was working on her laptop. Nicole went ahead and called in an emergency vacation so she wouldn't have to go into the doctor's office to try and get a work excuse. Actually, I would've been going, in her body. "She" has no signs of sickness so what would I be able to say on her behalf anyway? Oh, doc, I'm having an out of body experience and need a few days off? They'd put a notation in her records that she may be psychotic. That wouldn't be good at all. So, we decide to use this time to learn about each other since we don't know how long this will last.

"OK. So, we need to run down both of our schedules. Get on the same page about what we do and when we do it. And I need to walk you through everything I do at work. But first, I'm hungry. I'm going to go downstairs to this bistro and get us something to eat."

I get my bag of clothes and pull out something for her to put on. She changes, gets her debit card and starts to leave.

"I'm going to keep fasting a little bit longer. I'll eat something tomorrow."

"Suit yourself. I'll be back." She shrugs *my* shoulders and it doesn't look manly at all. I shake my head. I've got to give her a breakdown of how men do things, our mannerisms, mainly talking and movement, because she's not betraying me in the right light. She hesitates and peaks her head back through the door. "If you keep that up, I'll be able to fit into some of my old clothes."

When the door closes, I look down at her body. She has lost weight in these last few days. I've been officially fasting since Monday and I can already see the effects on her body, her slightly protruding stomach is gone, and I'm sure it's affected other parts of her body. Nicole has been fasting too, but just the Daniel fast. I'm going all in, what some would call a radical fast, but I need a radical breakthrough. This is not an easy process, but I am used to fasting to hear from God and understand his word clearly, so I can rightly divide it, to get direction as I serve his people, and before I make major decisions. I also fast just to be closer to God. I haven't eaten or drank anything since the meeting at my house Sunday afternoon. I wouldn't dare ask her to do this even though my body is used to it, because I know she doesn't have the willpower. I can tell her 'it's all in your mind' until the cows come home, but that's a decision you need to make on your own. I can't guilt her into it, God has to give her that desire if He so pleases. Even though I wish she would fast as I do, God's not going to honor her fast any less than He does mine.

While she's gone I start to write down everything I do each day. I go from Monday to Saturday. I don't want to even think about Sunday, so I skip it. I can't even imagine her pretending to be me in front of the congregation, speaking…preaching. I rub my forehead.

I didn't sign up for this. And I definitely don't want to spend my days at her office. I have too much other stuff to do. I have a church to run. I am curious what she does every day, but I don't want to be the one to do it. She has her computer here. She's going to have to work from home until we get this figured out. I hear the key turn in the front door.

"So, how do you want to do this?" I ask.

"Nicole, where have you been?"

"Huh!" I jump straight up. I don't know who this is but it's not me, it's not my body I'm looking at.

"You had me worried sick. I kept calling you. Why didn't you answer the phone?"

My mouth is wide open.

"Don't just stand there. Answer me. Your daddy told me not to come, but I knew something was wrong. But I get here and you're just sitting here all lackadaisical while you got us worried to death."

"Mother." I manage to speak out what my brain decoded, using the clues she just unwittingly gave me.

Her look changes. "Oh, something is wrong with you. Are you sick? You've never called me mother."

"Uh, yes." I try my best to cough and make myself look the part. Oh my. Lord, help me. What in the world is Nicole's mother doing here?

She looks me over. "You don't even look like yourself, like you've lost weight. Baby, you need to be in the bed. Forget about work. That's probably why you're sick now. Always working. If it 'aint for the job, it's for the church. You need to take a break every once in a while."

I'm too shocked to protest. I don't even know what to say or do so I just do what she says.

"I thought I locked the door but—Mamma!"

I can see Nicole's more terrified than I am as she steps inside.

"Well, what in the world? Yes, I'm Nicole's mother, and who are you?"

"I…"

"Mamma, that's my pastor, Pastor Darnell Thompson. I asked him to…bring me something to eat since I couldn't get up enough energy to—" My stomach decides to growl, cutting off my sentence.

"Thank you, Pastor." Nicole's mom gets up and takes the bag of food from her own daughter, housed in my shell.

We exchange a silent conversation with our eyes, as Nicole's mom unwraps the food.

What in the world do we do now?

I don't know it's your mom. Why didn't you call her back?

I didn't know she called. I haven't looked at my phone. I had more important things to think about don't you think!

"Pastor, thank you for bringing this. I'm here now. You can go."

"Well, we were discussing some important—"

"Is there something more important than my daughter's health, Pastor?" Nicole's mom has made it back to the bed and looks over her shoulder for an answer.

"Well, no ma'am." Nicole tries her best to impersonate me.

"So, you are a slave driver," her mom says under her breath.

"Excuse me?" I blurt out. I'm directing it to Nicole, because obviously they've had a conversation about me.

Her mom looks at me. "Nicole, I know you're not thinking straight, but you don't have to pretend."

"Mamma, I asked him to come. I need him to do a few things."

"Pastor Darren."

"It's Darnell."

"Excuse me, Pastor Darnell. I hear you run the church like you're a dictator."

I'm speechless.

"Don't look at Nicole. She may not tell you, but I don't have a problem saying something." Nicole looks at me then back to her mother. "So, you're not going to respond? That's fine. But I do want to thank you because you took the time to bring Nicole some food, although I don't know why she didn't call me. And to show my appreciation, I'd like you to come to our house for dinner. It'll give me and my husband a chance to get to know you better and see who Nicole is dealing with. It's always good to know who your child's spiritual leader is. Give Nicole time to get better first."

"No ma'am, that's very thoughtful of you but I can't," Nicole said.

"It's nothing special I'm always cooking, and you've got to eat anyway, might as well come get a home-cooked meal."

My temperature is rising. What does she mean by slave driver? What has Nicole been telling her, or anyone else?

"You can also let me and my husband know why you don't consider any of my daughter's ideas. She's very smart you know."

I'm looking at my own body, into my own eyes as they try to give a silent apology. But I don't want to hear it. I frown and look away.

"Actually, Pastor, that would be nice," I say. "Why don't you come by? Sounds like a nice discussion." With her mom's back still turned to me, I squint my eyes at Nicole. She has no doubt, I accepted the invitation to get her back. Let's see how she likes giving an explanation to her own parents about whatever complaints she's told them. How dare she talk about me, filling her parents' head with this nonsense. They're making judgements about me, based on their daughter's faulty point of view, and they don't even know me. I can see she's just like her mom too, trying to run something. But she can't handle me, nor control how I run my church. Let's see what her dad has to say. I wonder what else she's told them.

"Good, then it's settled. I'll let Nicole give you the details. I'll get her to eat. Thank you, Pastor and have a good day."

Nicole stammers for a moment, looks at me and I shrug my shoulders. "Nice to meet you ma'am," she says and leaves her own condo.

Nicole's mom looks at the salad and fruit. I can't eat that; my throat is raw. It'll burn going down. I've got to start slow, with just drinking some chicken broth. She can sense something is wrong.

"You want some soup instead?"

"I really don't feel like eating right now. I'll get some later."

"Come on Nicole, you need to eat so you can get your strength back. I'll go make you some soup. I know you should have at least one can in there if you still do like I've taught you. I've always told you to keep at least one can of chicken noodle soup, because you never know when you'll need it."

I know she won't leave until she sees me eat something, so I acquiesce. "I'd rather have just chicken broth if there's some in there."

"Nicole, you really are sick…broth?"

About fifteen minutes later she returns with a bowl of broth and crackers. She tries to feed me, but I tell her I can do it myself. Well, so much for my fast. God knows my heart. I was planning on ending it tomorrow anyway. She gives me the spoon and waits until she sees me swallow. This gives her assurance I will finish the bowl, so she feels my forehead.

"You don't have a fever. That's good."

"Yeah, I think I'm getting over it now. I really just need to get some sleep."

"That's right baby, I'll go so you can get your rest. Call me if you need anything…And why did you call him and not your own mamma, after all he's put you through?"

"Because that's probably why I'm sick now, overworked at the church, so I figure he owes that to me." Sure, I can play along.

"You're absolutely right. But you just need to say no to some things. They'll work you to the bone, you're the one that's got to speak up. If you can't do something, you just can't do it. You're going to run yourself ragged. Let somebody else do it for a change."

I slowly shake my head. "Oh, I promise you Mamma, I will."

***

Nicole comes back up after I call her. We wait a good twenty minutes after her mom leaves, just to make sure she doesn't resurface.

"Slave driver, what was that all about?"

"Yeah, I told my mom a few things I didn't like about you. I was frustrated. I didn't think it'd ever get back to you."

"Why didn't you just tell me?"

"You don't listen to what I tell you already."

"Listening and agreeing are two different things." I sigh. "Well, now she sees me in a negative light."

She shrugs. "At least I didn't discuss it with anyone at the church. Why did you agree to dinner?"

"I'm curious to know what else you've said about me behind my back."

"That's family. That doesn't count. Odds are they would have never met you."

"It doesn't matter about not meeting me. People talk to other people. Who knows how many other people she's told that to. I can get a bad reputation just like that."

"OK, look, let's just get back to going over our routines."

"Fine."

After debriefing, I must admit we learned quite a bit about each other. She does do a lot. Her schedule is pretty tight after working eight to nine hours every day, commuting an hour to and from work, with traffic, not to mention being a Sunday school teacher over the middle schoolers, leader over the women's ministry, and my secretary at the church. I don't know how she finds time for it all.

"If you're doing too much, why do you sign up for it?"

"Because no one else will do it. People say they're going to do it but they're not consistent, so I end up doing it."

I don't have an answer for this.

"So, you run a few errands here and there and have a few conference calls with other ministers. But otherwise you're free the whole day?" she asks.

"No. I'm not free. Did you miss that I pray and study the word, plan out my sermons and bible-study teachings, and strategize for the church? That doesn't even include dealing with other people's issues that come up."

"You actually study for hours at a time?"

"Several, yes; beyond when I study for what I'm going to preach or teach about. Why do you find that so hard to believe?"

"I don't know."

"We need to avoid what just happened with your mom. I need to know everyone in your immediate family."

I scroll down her contact favorites and study the pictures of her family and close friends as she points them out and gives me the details. We just go over the most pertinent ones, who I may run into.

"I won't answer your phone unless I have to. I'll just send text messages back if they leave a message," I say.

"Good idea, me too."

She scrolls to the next name and points. Her phone rings and she jumps. "Oh no, that's Terrance."

"Terrance?"

"My boyfriend." She pushes the red decline button.

"Don't you think you need to answer it? We don't need a repeat of your mother."

"I know. I know. I don't know what to say though."

"Tell him the same thing I told your mom."

"No, no. He may try and come up here too."

"He still will if you don't talk to him."

"You do realize you're the one that's got to talk to him."

"Oh, right."

"I'll text him. I'll say I'm in a meeting."

"I didn't know you were seeing someone."

"You don't know anything about me."

"It's just a thought. I didn't mean anything by it."

"What, you thought I wanted to be your secretary to get next to you? Please, I'm not like some of these other women."

"What do you mean by that?"

"Pastor Darnell, are you serious? Open your eyes. There are a lot of women at church who are only there because they want to get a piece of an eligible bachelor."

"Why would they want to date a pastor? My life might be considered boring by most people's standards."

"My thoughts exactly. But some women still want to get with you."

"Why?"

"Because you have something they want, position and power. If they get with you that automatically elevates their status in the church."

"I don't have time for that. I'll just put on a wedding ring then."

"Huh, that may make it worse."

"What do you mean?"

"A wedding ring will make some of them want you more?"

"That makes no sense."

"Pastor, you're so naïve. It's called forbidden fruit."

"I'm talking about my members not people in the streets."

"I'm talking about your members too. Don't you think for one minute, all the women in the church are just there because they love the Lord. They're trying to get close to you."

"I don't recall anyone trying to come on to me or anything."

"Oh no, they'll be more subtle. They'll ask around first, to see what information they can get on you."

"Has anyone ever asked you—"

"Yep." She answers before I can finish. "Some of them feel threatened by me and think I want you, but I set them straight. I tell them I'm in a relationship and the pastor isn't even my type. Then they think they can get close to me to get in good with you. I know the game."

Hmm. "Well, thank you. Because I don't need the distraction."

"You're welcome but it's like I'm seeing the same thing all over again. I saw it with Pastor Andrews. They didn't dare try that mess while Sister Andrews was alive because she didn't play that. She was a wise woman and knew exactly what she was up against. But after she passed away, her body wasn't in the ground good before women showed their true colors and came out of the woodwork. And they don't even know what they're setting themselves up for, scheming to get with the pastor. Being married to a pastor is no cake-walk. And if you do end up marrying a pastor, being the First Lady just means you will be the next target. Someone's always going to criticize you and someone's always going to be trying to get next to your husband. You've got to always be on your guard. But I've got to hand it to Pastor Andrews, he was wise too and he always praised his wife and made sure to honor her publicly. He could have remarried after she passed but he never did."

I shake my head and dial back in to get any basic information I may need about Terrance. "How long have you two been dating?"

"Two years."

"Oh, great."

"What?"

"Then he's definitely gonna want to see you. I'm not doing that. You need to figure something out to keep him away. Who else do I need to know?"

She points to the last name of importance. "My sister Trina, stands for Trinity. We don't talk often, maybe once a week, she's busy with her life, and me with mine, but we text each other a lot." She sits back, done with her spiel. "Any texts you think are important, just forward them to me and I'll send you a response to text back to them. Anything else we'll deal with at night."

I shake my head and we repeat the process with my side. She already knows all the people from church who may call me, even ministers at other churches that I talk to. The only other people are my family, who don't even live in Houston, they all live in Atlanta, but I run down the short list of my mom, dad, and brother anyway.

"That was a lot of information," I say, reviewing my notes.

"What about church tonight?" she asks.

"We just won't go. I'll get one of the other ministers to fill in."

"Why not just cancel it?"

"No, you got to keep the people in their routine. If they miss one bible study, it'll be that much easier to miss the next one, and before you know it, you don't see them in months. No, it's important to stick to the schedule."

"But you can go. I don't do much on Wednesdays unless you ask me to. Normally I just sit and listen to you teach."

"I'm not ready for that yet. One thing at a time."

# 12 Nicole

I'M AWOKEN WITH a hand on my shoulder shaking me to get up. I turn and look at the clock. It's 5am Sunday morning. And I'm about to cry because I'm staring at my body, hovering over me. My own eyes are looking at me; the realization that I'm still stuck in this foreign body.

Pastor Darnell studied all week like he would be preaching this morning. He acted in faith. So did I. Now what? We'll have to skip Sunday service.

"Sunday is when everything happened. I thought for sure today we'd be back ourselves."

"Me too." He drops his head. "Listen, I need you to call Minister Donnie, so he can preach this morning." Let me write down some things you can say. And just pick whatever feels comfortable based on his response."

I get situated as Pastor jots down a few lines that I read aloud to practice and see how I sound. We don't have much time. We need to call him sooner than later, to give him all the time he needs to prepare something. I feel bad for Donnie, I'd be a nervous wreck if I got a call the morning of, to preach. I exhale and dial the number from pastor's phone.

"Put him on speaker phone so I can hear."

I sit up to the edge of the couch and swallow. "Remember you can't say anything. You've got my voice and if he hears you—" He nods his understanding. The phone rings twice, then goes to voicemail. "Uh, he rejected your call."

"Hang up and call him again. Don't leave any voicemails."

The phone rings forever then goes to voicemail again. Pastor starts pacing the floor. He's biting on the side of my nails, which is annoying because I know I don't have any hangnails. He can mess up my cuticles.

"If he doesn't answer I can call a couple more people, but I may get the same result. Besides, I'd prefer he do it. And I definitely don't want to call any of my fellow pastors. They need to get ready for their own churches. And if I ask for one of their ministers to fill in for me, that'll make me look bad; to be in this position for one and secondly because that means I don't have any capable ministers in my own church who can teach when I'm not there."

I don't know what to say so I remain silent. He leaves and comes back after about ten minutes and sits back down. "Try him again." I do and on the fourth ring, he answers. I hear the sleep still in his voice. I explain that I'm really sick and need him to preach. And I say, "I apologize. I hate to spring this on you like this." If he was sleep, he's definitely wide awake now. He says he has nothing prepared with such short notice. But I remind him that a minister should always have a word. That's something our old pastor used to say. I can hear him scrambling on the other end of the phone. In the end he tells me that I can count on him to get it done, and that's all Pastor and I want to hear.

With a temporary reprieve, now we've got to refocus our thoughts on Monday morning. Pastor may have someone to fill in for *him,* but I don't have that luxury. I've been away from the office an entire week and my boss needs to see me in person. Darnell's got to do it. I've just got to teach him how.

"OK. Well, you've got to learn how to be me because I've got to be at work tomorrow."

He clearly doesn't like it, but he gives me little resistance. We go over my work schedule again and what needs to be done when. I show him the programs he needs to access to pull reports and who to give them to.

"Why can't you just do your work from your laptop here?"

"Because they track everything. They know when I log on and from where. If they see my computer logging into a company system across town and know I'm in the office, that will raise red flags because it's impossible for me to be in two places at one time."

"Then just work entirely from home."

"I can't. That's only allowed for emergencies—"

"This definitely qualifies!"

"And, I have limited functionality from my laptop. Most of what needs to be done can only be done from the systems set up in the office. Now will you stop with the stall tactics? If there was another way, believe me, I'd do it."

His head falls into his hand and he starts rubbing his forehead, understanding the enormity of the task. He probably did get the short end of the stick because all I basically have to do being him, is read and pray and let the ministers take over until he gets back in his own body. But that's not my fault, I didn't ask for this.

I open my laptop and pour out a flood of information. I print out a pictorial organization chart, so he can associate my coworkers' pictures with their names. We spend the next couple of hours going over everything he'll need to do this week.

"Now come with me. I've already got my clothes lined out for the week, so you don't have to think about what you're going to wear each day, however long this lasts."

I point to each outfit and match the shoes to go with each, to make it easier. Then I go to my dresser and return with the correct undergarments to wear with each, which I place on the hanger of each outfit. I don't trust him not to wear a red bra underneath a thin white shirt.

"Man, I'm not playing dress-up. Can't you wear some slacks and a collared shirt to work?"

I tilt my head back and take a deep breath. "Pastor Darnell, there is a certain standard in my office. The men wear ties and slacks and add suit jackets when we're meeting with clients. And the women normally wear dresses and skirts. And I have a certain standard for myself, so I dress very nice and I mostly wear heels."

"I hope you have some slacks in there. If not, you need to buy some because I'm not wearing a skirt. I don't go that way."

"I'm not questioning your manhood. Just think of it as a kilt." His chest rises. "Or shorts with no separator," I offer.

"You can say what you want, I'm not doing it."

He can pout all he wants but he really doesn't have a choice. I try to get him to focus on something else. "Well at least let me show you how to walk in heels, in case you need to do it if my boss wants you to meet a client or someone from corporate comes into the office."

I pick up Monday's black three-and-a-half-inch pair of stilettos and hand it to him. I offer my arm for support, but he elects to use the door frame. He stands back up and tilts his head as if to say, *Are you satisfied?* I grin. "Now walk," I command.

He takes a deep breath and starts going. I count backward in my head, *three, two, one* and as I suspect, he wobbles, twists his ankle, and frantically grasps at air as he falls. What a sight. I hold my laughter in though because anything at this point could send him over the edge. I quickly help him up. I'm staring into eyes that are blaring into my soul. I only have a limited time before I lose him. I switch into teacher mode and show him how to walk as I hold on to my own body. I can sense the competitiveness in him. He refuses to give me the satisfaction of seeing him fail, so we keep walking until he's mastered it.

"OK, I did it." He takes them off and looks down the array of colors, all of them having heels, and says to himself, "you don't have any flats?" Before I can answer, he's rummaging through the closet and finds some tennis shoes. "Yes," he says with satisfaction. I still don't say anything, but he keeps looking. In the back of the closet, he finds his prize, not one but two sets of flats. I haven't worn them in years. They just don't give off the same vibe as heels do.

I've got to reel him back in. "If you don't wear the heels, you'll cause more attention to yourself because wearing flats is something I just don't do. It's not me. People will notice because I'm not acting normal."

"Well, you called in sick, so when you go back to work, you don't have to act normal."

I scrunch the side of my mouth. "You dress at the level you want to become. Haven't you ever heard that? This is my career you're playing with. Aren't you being selfish? I'd do something I don't like for you if I had to."

"And thank God you don't. We've got enough ministers to handle that," he smirks.

I feel my temperature rise. He doesn't think I can do it. He thinks his job is so important...well it is, but I can do what he does, for a little while at least.

"Look, Darnell, I'm in a position at work where I can't afford any mishaps. This emergency vacation is already a negative data point, because we're supposed to turn vacation requests in at least two weeks in advance and I don't need to have any reason for me to be overlooked for important assignments that can advance my career. You *will* do everything that I would do, exactly like I would, including wearing what I wear."

We have a stare down, but he knows I'm serious. I fold my arms, daring him to try and back out of this. I don't even blink. He turns and leaves the room as I silently call him every name I can think of in my head. When he returns he says, "OK Nicole, I don't want to jeopardize your career. I'll do it."

"And wear the clothes?"

"Yes."

"Including the heels?"

He breathes in deeply. "Yes."

"Thank you very much," I reply.

"Let's take a break from talking about your responsibilities. Let's go over my typical week again," he says.

"Again? I don't think I need another debrief. I'm sure I can figure it out. You're a fairly simple man. If I have any questions, I'll call you."

"Right," he slowly shakes his head, "if you say so." And if I'm not mistaken, he seems to be holding in a smile.

# 13 Darnell

I PULL INTO the parking lot of Nicole's job and replace the flats for heels. Over the phone, Nicole directs me through the procedures of entering the building and getting inside the offices. She tells me the names of the pertinent people again just before I enter. I walk into the establishment and find her office. I double check the name outside the door and unlock it. I barely have time to set down my things when Jenny enters, right on cue, just as Nicole had mentioned she would.

"What are you doing?" she smirks.

I quickly retrace my steps. I did walk into the correct office because the key worked. What did Nicole forget to tell me? "What do you mean?"

"Why are you walking like that?"

"Like what?"

"Like a cartoon character, or a stick figure. It's like you're walking forward but leaning back at the same time."

"Oh, I had back surgery." Why did I say that? Relax Darnell, be cool.

"Back surgery?"

"I mean, it felt like back surgery. I went to a chiropractor and I—"

"Well honey, you need to get that fixed. You just look silly. See you in a bit."

*Lord, you're just gonna have to forgive me. I'm trying to survive here. I don't know what may come out of my mouth.* I look at the silver wall clock. She must be talking about the morning meeting which will start in over an hour. I practiced walking in heels with Nicole again this morning. She said I did fine. I don't know what happened in that length of time, but I need to figure this out. I close the door and put my back against the wall, making sure my shoulders are back and my body is straight. I concentrate and walk around her office. Then I go to the break room and watch all the women walk. I look at their shoes. There are a few who have taller heels than she does. I don't think they're even appropriate for a place of business; they're going overboard. I've got to hand it to Nicole, at least hers are at a professional height. I commit their strides to memory and go to the women's restroom and practice again. I watch myself in the wall-to-wall mirrors. I do this repeatedly until I mimic their movements. *I was an athlete this can't be this hard.* I study my movements. *It's almost like staying in ready position, on the balls of your feet so you can move in any direction in a split second,* I surmise. OK, now I've got it down.

I grab Nicole's portfolio and enter the conference room. I decline Jenny's coffee offer but save her a seat next to me. If something is said that I don't understand, I need to be able to whisper my question to her.

"You're walking normal again, what did you do?"

"Oh, I stretched my back."

She nodded her approval. Many people trickle into the room and say hello to me. There are a few private conversations about what they did over the weekend, their child's upcoming activity, or the weekend game, but everything comes to a halt when one man enters. I recognize him as Nicole's boss, by the picture she showed me on the company website, which I realize now is a little outdated. I'd give Gary 5 feet 10, but his face is rounder than what I saw and his stomach matches. He talks a good thirty minutes about the state of the business and with my sales background I can follow along pretty well. Actually, I fit in just fine. I've just got to work the kinks out. A few people around the table ask a few questions and make comments, but I don't dare say anything. I just continue to take notes. The meeting officially adjourns, and a few side conversations start up again. Gary looks my way. "Glad to have you back, Nicole. Let's debrief in my office."

Nicole already prepared me for this. She wrote down bulleted notes for each client and walked me through the questions he will ask. As I walk toward Gary, he asks me how my vacation was, and did I do anything special. I realize that with all the information

Nicole and I went over we didn't discuss what I would say if someone asked. I smile as my mind tries to come up with something believable because Nicole's "vacation" was supposedly unplanned and started out as sick time.

"Well—" I start to answer when my foot turns and to keep from falling I instinctively grab Gary's arm which makes him spill his cup of coffee on his crisp white button-down long-sleeve shirt and of course it didn't miss his red and white striped tie, which now sports brown stripes as well. He groans because of the temperature of the coffee on his skin. My knee almost touches the floor, but I pull myself up. You can light up a stadium as big as my eyes are shining. "I am so sorry. I don't know what happened." My eyes dart to my feet and I move them to survey the area. There's a small kink protruding out of the carpet that I hadn't noticed before. It had snagged my heel. I can tell I twisted my ankle. I grab some nearby napkins and give them to Gary who is unsuccessfully patting himself dry. Now he's rubbing the coffee stains and the napkins are breaking apart and leaving crumples of wet paper on his clothes. I can feel the eyes of the others in the room on me. I don't look back; their silence speaks enough. Gary asks me to give him a minute while he goes to the bathroom to try and get the stains out.

I head straight for Nicole's office and close the door. I won't dare tell Nicole; I won't give her the satisfaction. She already thinks I can't handle something as simple as walking in heels. I was doing fine. It's like working out your calf muscles. I just didn't know something as simple as a thread of carpet, that was probably pulled out by an old vacuum cleaner, can mess you up, but I'm on the lookout now. I've got this.

# 14 Nicole

I FEEL LIKE I'm eating every few minutes. I'm trying to keep my mind off of my job and concentrate on the pastoral job I'm supposed to be doing for Darnell, but I find myself looking at the time often during the day and wondering what he's doing, and how he's interacting with my coworkers. How is he acting in the morning meeting? I told him to be accessible for my boss, but don't go in his office uninvited. The more he can stay under the radar, the better. Can anyone tell the difference? If anyone can tell something is wrong, it will be Jenny, and I warned him of that.

He calls me a couple of times, but we only talk long enough for him to ask me specific questions on how to do something. His text messages, which I quickly answer back, are asking about what particular acronyms mean. He probably has little time to think about what I'm doing.

The cell phone rings again and it's him. "How are things going?" I ask.

"OK. I had to ask Jenny a few things. She knows something's not right with you, but she's been understanding. I researched some potential clients your boss gave me this morning. It brought back memories of my old sales job. There are some presentations that I put a rough shell on, but you'll have to add the meat and potatoes."

I match his abrupt let's-get-down-to-business tone and address his concerns in rapid succession. "That's fine…No problem…Right…In the top drawer…Just remember to bring my laptop back." From an observer's perspective we sound like an auctioneer and bidder, but my question breaks the chant. "Why didn't you tell me you had all these interruptions during the day?"

"That goes along with the life of a simple man, didn't you know?"

"OK. I was wrong for saying that. But you could have told me from the beginning, that you'd have all these calls. You just told me about the pastor calls you have scheduled, and you wrote notes for those, but these other calls—"

"Well, why did you answer?"

"I didn't. I'm listening to all the voicemails people are leaving you. Do you want me to call them back?"

"Yes, that's fine. Any ones you can't handle, leave for me and I'll tell you what to do. I've got to go; I have another meeting."

He quickly hangs up, but I don't mind. I know all too well how busy he is and will continue to be up until the last few minutes before he steps out of the office and shuts down for the day. It's just the way the industry is. The nature of the business of connecting people with the right job opportunity and fulfilling a customer's laundry list of open positions which contain detailed requirements, is an art. It often requires long hours but is very rewarding.

As I sit on my couch, the words 'you can't handle' keep replaying in my mind. I *can* handle these calls, maybe not the way he would, but I can handle them, and I'll show him I can. I don't need his help; it's not rocket science. For the next hour, I get a game plan together to address every problem each person has dealt me today and start returning calls.

# 15 Nicole

I WAKE UP again hoping that I'm now myself. *Please God* is my only thought when I open my eyes. The first thing I do is feel my chest and all I can grab is a fist full of hair. I snatch the covers back and see my body looking at me.

I vocalize my frustration. "What we're doing is not working. There's something we're supposed to get out of this and until we embrace it, I don't know how long we'll be like this."

"What do you mean embrace it?" he asks.

"I mean me be completely you and you be completely me. We need to live exactly like the other person does. Go all in, which means we've got to stop taking showers together."

"But our eyes are closed. I'm bathing my own body and you're bathing your own. We don't need to see each other's body, Nicole. We should keep it like that."

"It's not practical. Look, you know what a woman's body looks like. Get over yourself. Stop trying to be holier than thou. And this isn't the first time I've seen a naked man."

"No, I was trying to be respectful."

"OK. Well, I appreciate that, but we've got to actually live separately. For one, my condo's not going to let me have someone over here for an extended period of time when you're not on the lease. Believe me they're watching. And how does it look that a pastor hasn't been seen out of his house, inside his house, nor anywhere near it. I'm sure your neighbors pretty much know your routine, but they haven't seen you. The last thing we need is the police showing up at your doorstep for a welfare check."

"Alright, You're right. Since we're going all in, that's probably what we need to do. But we're still staying the course with the church, right?"

I shake my head. "Pastor, I don't like this anymore than you do but I really think I'm supposed to do everything that you do."

"Awe, come on. You've got to be kidding."

"What other choice do we have? You want to stay in my body any longer than you have to? I think the sooner we do this, the sooner we get this over with."

He lifts his hand over his forehead and scratches his head, which doesn't have the same effect when doing it in a woman's body.

"Alright. Fine."

I start in on the details. "OK. Things you need to know. You've got to put a cap on my hair when you shower, or it'll get frizzy."

"What does it matter, when you wear a wig anyway?"

"That's just on bad hair days. Just make it a practice to always wear a shower cap. And when you shower, only use that one soap. There's only so many kinds that don't irritate me down low so stick to the one already in there. So, what about you?"

"I don't have any rules. You can do what you want."

"That's what I mean by 'simple man'. Fair enough."

He smiles, and we get ready for him to drive me back to his house.

# 16 Darnell

I ARRIVE AT church and do my normal walk through around and am greeted by one of the youth teachers. "Sister Nicole, you mind bringing me up to speed with what you taught your class on your Sunday?"

"Sure." Nicole told me this might happen. Sis. Florence, one of the kids' bible study teachers, would on occasion ask Nicole for the notes and scriptures of what she taught for Sunday School so Sis. Florence could reteach it for bible study on Wednesday. "But I wasn't here last Sunday, and it wasn't my turn to teach."

"That's OK, tell me about the last lesson you *did* teach." She's holding the bathroom door open for me and when I don't move she says, "You mind; I just want to retouch my make-up?"

I'm about to tell her I can't tonight when I hear my name in the background. Well, not my name but my title, pastor. I can't see, but someone behind the door says it, so I decide to walk in.

"Just give me a few seconds to powder my nose."
She sets her books in one of the chairs and hurries
toward the mirror."

Now I can see and hear the source of my name
dropping. It's two women. The fact that they are
talking about me causes me to sit in one of the chairs.
I choose the seat next to Sis. Florence's things. I've
seen both women in a handful of services before but
they're not members and I have no idea what their
names are and they're not saying them either. The one
with the tight skirt, whom I'll call Lady X, quickly
hunches Lady Y to be quiet. They still don't call each
other's names out though, which I believe is
intentional. I can hear Lady X say under her breath,
"that's the pastor's secretary."

Lady Y says, "Oh, it's okay she's cool." She then
turns back to Lady X and says, "You'd better go
ahead and make your move while he's still single."

Lady X says, "He doesn't have to be single. If I
want them, I'm going to get them regardless."

I cringe at her choice of words. She has obviously
practiced this on other men and "gotten" them, as she
puts it. She obviously has no respect for couples'
relationships. I'm looking at a homewrecker, and they
are busy looking at the mirror while putting on
lipstick.

Lady Y asks Lady X, "How do you plan to get his
attention?"

Lady X responds with, "These will get his
attention," and pushes up her breasts to reveal more
cleavage.

Lady Y screams and I turn to see why. I witness my body enter the door brandishing red cheeks and fumbling words. Nicole looks at me and I'm just as surprised as she is. She apologizes and leaves just as quickly as she appeared, but the talking continues.

"Girl, what on earth is Pastor thinking, barging into the women's restroom?" Lady Y asks.

"That must be a sign. I think about him and he appears!"

"Did you just see what the pastor had on? He's either got a tailor or he is trying to impress someone."

"And I think I'm his inspiration," Lady X says.

"He's definitely dressing better than he ever has before."

"Yes. The clothes make him look even more handsome."

I can't believe what I'm hearing. Nicole is right. No matter what I do or don't do, I'm still the focus of attention for some women, especially those not coming to church for the right reason.

# 17 Nicole

IT'S WEDNESDAY NIGHT and I drive into the church parking lot and grab Pastor's bible and my notes off the passenger's seat. Pastor, as they know it, looks a little different. I wonder if anyone will notice. I didn't do anything drastic, just a few tweaks. I walk a few steps inside the front door. "Wow, Pastor you sure put that outfit together, do you have a new stylist?" Sis Brenda asks.

*OK. That's definitely a yes.* "No, Sis Brenda, just making a few changes, that's all."

"I've never seen you in ripped jeans before."

"Is it too much?"

"No, no. You look fashionable and it's tasteful. I like it."

"What about the shirt?"

"Love, the shirt. It's nice to see you wearing something other than…earth tones."

I thank her then proceed to pastor's office. I place my things on his desk and walk around to check on the youth classrooms before service starts. A few children give me hugs and I say hello to the teachers. I pick up empty peppermint wrappers off the floor and I pass by the bathroom and check to make sure all the supplies are stocked up. A scream jolts me out of my rhythm. All the women become statues except one whose hands are on both sides of her head. She jerks once, clearly adjusting her wig, then puts her hands to her side. It takes me a second or so to even comprehend what the problem is. It seems they're looking at me, so I turn to the ladies sitting in the lounge chairs and see my own body, with the same look as the other women, mouth wide open.

"Oh, oh. Right. Sorry, I was, uh, wrong bathroom." I retreat as quickly as a turtle vanishes into its shell when prodded. I can't rely on habit. I've got to really focus on who I am right now, at all times, so something like that doesn't happen again. I walk away fast and make my way to the sanctuary.

I sit in the front and gather my thoughts. I mentally shake off the blunder and concentrate on the task before me. I open my bible and peruse through my notes. As I look at my watch, I hear a loud thud and I see my body hold onto one of the doors as if holding it would erase the sound it just made. The bathroom mix-up was a blur, so I get a chance to really look at myself walk in. I immediately look at my feet and see Pastor is not wearing heels, which is fine. I had told him flats were appropriate, but he didn't do that either. Even his choice of tennis shoes would have been O.K. if he hadn't decided to dress my body in some old sweats. Not only do they represent the apparel of the eighties era, they also have a few discolored spots and bleach stains on them. Who does that? Sure, they're minuscule, but if someone is really paying attention, they can see them. I wouldn't be caught dead in those clothes. He had to have found that in the bottom of my drawer. I just wear them on cold days inside my condo with my thickest pair of socks. *Does he not pay any attention at all to the way I dress or is he doing this on purpose?*

I drop my head and pinch the top of my nose. I don't want to call any more attention to who everyone thinks is me, so I get started. In bible study I fill up the time with more of asking the participants questions and having them think as opposed to me just teaching. I'm used to dividing the time into games, teaching, and crafts with my Sunday School class because of their attention span. Tonight, I'm taking a page from what I know so for part of the lesson, I split the adults into groups.

After service concludes Pastor Darnell and I decide it best for him to leave and for me to stay and lock the church up with the other brothers and to call each other on the way home. I call him as soon as I leave the parking lot and start in as soon as he answers the phone.

"Why did you do that?"

"Do what?"

"Don't have me coming to church looking any kind of way. Don't have me anywhere looking any kind of way."

"Nicole, I didn't wear that today. After I left your job I changed."

"Why?"

"So I can be comfortable. You've got layers of clothes on plus panty hose. I can't wear that stuff that long. You're used to it, I'm not."

"You better pull it together. You've never seen me wear something like that. You could have at least put me on something that looks better than that. You could have worn jeans and a shirt with those tennis shoes, and I would have been fine but come on!"

"You need to loosen up a bit."

"The outfit I just described, *is* loosening up a bit, but you went way left field with the gray sweats. And how could you not see the stains?"

"What stains?"

"At the bottom of the sleeves and down by the ankles."

He's quiet for a moment; it's probably the first time he's even really looked at what he put on.

"If someone is able to see these, they're looking too hard."

I throw my hands up. "Don't even worry about it. Just never wear that again." I shake my head and continue. "Are you color blind?"

"Yes. And I wish all of us were, so we can really love our brother the way we're supposed to."

I feel lines form on my forehead. "No, I'm not talking spiritually, but for real, I mean medically. Are you medically color-blind?"

"No, I see perfectly. What makes you think that?"

"Because you hardly have any clothes with color in it."

"That's not what I'm about?"

"What, looking good?"

"There's nothing wrong with the way I look. I just don't want to draw any attention to myself. It's just not my focus. My focus is on God. Speaking of, I like the way you taught tonight. You got more people engaged. Well done."

I thank him, and we talk about my job and what he's doing tomorrow at the agency. We pray and hope things are back to normal tomorrow, for obvious reasons, let alone the fact that we have to fulfill my mother's invitation of having the pastor over for dinner.

# 18 Darnell

I PULL UP to Nicole's parents' house. The red brick is outlined by dark brown trim and the one story seems to sit on a sea of green; the grass is so thick. I park in the driveway and go over in my head, the things Nicole and I have talked about, among which I've got to remember to call her mom, Mamma and her dad, Daddy.

We both decide it best to come separately but to pull up almost at the same time, so I don't do anything out of sorts without her being here to coach me. Even though Nicole told me some things to say and do I don't think a person knows the subtle nuances that govern how they express themselves with family, so I have no idea how she normally behaves in her parents' home. I go along with this now, even though I'm not myself, because her mom invited me, so I don't want to offend her by ignoring the invitation, and she's not the type of woman you ignore. That will just give her more to talk about. And from what I've heard up to now, Nicole has given her enough questionable material on me already. So, here's my chance as a pastor to redeem myself in Nicole's mom's eyes. I've drilled Nicole on what to talk about, so now I want to get this over with. It's going to be interesting to see how Nicole handles being me, since now she's got to overcome the negative persona of me that *she* created with her parents. All I have to do is sit back and watch.

Nicole pulls up and I look over myself one more time, hoping that I've satisfied her wardrobe requirements for the occasion. I avoided her dresser and took clothes only from what was hanging in her closet. I searched until I'd found a t-shirt and jeans, and I paired them with some dark brown loafers. I figure, since I'm her, I can't really go too wrong here as far as her parents are concerned. What would they say to their own daughter about what she decides to wear at her own parents' house? I'm sure her father doesn't care, and I've never met him. Her mother on the other hand, may be picky but she'll be too busy trying to keep her eye on who she thinks is me. My concern is satisfying Nicole's high standards.

We get out of our vehicles at the same time and my body walks over to me. She raises an eyebrow and shrugs her shoulder, a reluctant acceptance of my choice of clothes on *her* body. On the other hand, I'm looking at someone who just stepped out of a modeling magazine. Nicole can really put a wardrobe together. A blue button-down short sleeve shirt with multi-colored speckles, camel-brown pants and what I say are orange oxford shoes, yet she corrects me and says the color is actually called glazed ginger. She found clothes I have forgotten I own, and I never would have thought to put them together, but they work, even with the orange shoes she bought.

I lead the way up the path, like I know what I'm doing. Although I have her keys, Nicole has to point out which one opens the front door. We walk into what looks like a model home. It is so inviting. Nothing is cluttered, everything is perfectly coordinated. There's even an accent wall. I only know this terminology from over hearing remodeling shows that happen to be playing as I sit in the waiting room at doctor appointments. I can only assume this is the work of Nicole's mother. She is as good with staging, as Nicole is with wardrobes. She got it honestly.

I observe all this quickly though because since I'm Nicole, I'm supposed to be the one guiding and introducing "me" to Nicole's father. Nicole plays her part and stands back a little, pretending to see the place for the first time, and comments on the artwork that adorn the walls. I remember my role and hug both her parents while I present them to my pastor, all while explaining my protection for them is the reason I'm not kissing them (as Nicole normally does). Getting over this pretend sickness is proving to be very useful. Her mom ignores my rationalization and plants one on my cheek anyway.

What I didn't expect were two additional people. My eyes widen as a woman and man walk into the room. Nicole told me the names of her family, but I don't want to get this wrong. I quickly turn to Nicole for help as I say, "And Pastor, these are…"

She blurts out, "Kenny and Trina!"

That was a bit much, and all their faces agree with me, so she has to clean it up a bit. Seeing her siblings is a surprise, which means there are more eyes on me, (well who they think is me).

Dinner is fantastic; Mrs. Freeman can really cook. We have good conversation and Nicole does very well impersonating me, although she gets tripped up on a couple questions that I have to cleverly guide her through. Those don't concern me, what does is that in their eyes, I am the one who sprays soda from my mouth, across the table. It's partially my fault. I eat the same amount I normally eat as a man, but I'm not in my own body, so for a woman getting a hefty helping of seconds on everything, including a good amount of meat, I really messed up. Nicole's mom is staring me down and doesn't mix words. How does it look when you ask your daughter if she's pregnant, and her pastor is the one who reacts? I can't believe what I'm seeing. Nicole is frazzled. All of this is unsettling, and I can sense an uneasiness from her brother.

After dinner, I get the privilege of washing dishes with Nicole's sister as I watch my body leave when invited to the other room. Nicole's brother joins Nicole and their dad. To Nicole's credit, she does insist on staying and helping clean the dishes with us, which would help me overcome any issues I have with the female conversations, but Mr. Freeman won't hear of that. I do think I score some points with Mrs. Freeman for the gesture though. She comes in and out of the kitchen while me and Nicole's sister clean up. I don't want Trinity to sense anything, so I play around with her just like I would my own brother. I try to avoid her asking me anything, because I probably don't know the answers, and try to keep her talkative by asking her a bunch of questions about how her job is going, her love life, etc., and any information she gives me, I milk it for all it's worth. I mean every piece of detail I follow it down like it's a rabbit trail. When she mentions she needs to get her breaks fixed, I talk about the new car models, the different colors, and prices. I probably sound ridiculous, but I've got to do anything possible to avoid being tripped up by a question or a memory I don't know.

When we're finished with all the clean-up, Nicole's mom comes back in the kitchen. And as Trinity leaves to join the others, I follow suit. That is until Mrs. Freeman pulls me to the side.

"Nicole, let me talk to you for a minute."

"Yes, ma'am." I can't go wrong with that answer.

She doesn't waste any words as she lowers her voice. "Nicole, don't think I didn't see those men's clothes on top of the bag when I was in your condo. I raised you better than that."

I swallow hard, searching for an explanation, but I'm caught off guard, so none comes.

"I might have been born at night, but I wasn't born last night. Tell Terrance to stay at his own place. You don't play house with anyone."

I don't respond, well with words anyway. But my non-response is automatically a guilty response. She walks off and leaves me alone with what is supposed to be my guilt, but I'm not Nicole so her admonishment falls on the wrong ears.

I wait a while before I go into the living room, hopefully giving Nicole's mom some satisfaction that she has gotten through to her daughter. I'm relieved that at least she doesn't think those clothes belong to me. There's no coming back from that. Even though Nicole and I are only a few years apart, and people all over the world are fornicating left and right, even Christians, this is unacceptable behavior for a pastor, under any circumstances. And any church would crucify their leader if they got wind of anything of the sort.

Nicole seems to be having a good time talking to her father and brother about the game. I observe for a while. *Talk about an out-of-body experience.* Having to see someone in your own body pretend to be you while surrounded by their own flesh and blood family is surreal. We stay another thirty minutes, then I initiate our dismissal.

# 19 Nicole

I PULL UP to my parent's home and park behind Darnell. We're quizzing each other on the phone all the way over here and both add last minute facts we think may come in handy as we walk up to the front door. I ring the doorbell once and show him the key to open the front door. I can smell the food as soon as the door opens. I can't help but smile.

I hunch Darnell and whisper, "Tell them we're here. Remember, act like me."

"We're in the kitchen," my mom yells back.

Before we can walk to the kitchen, we're greeted by my parents, but then my brother and sister pop up and I abruptly stop. I'm caught off guard, so I blurt out their nicknames, which Darnell shouldn't know. The shock draws it out of me. I am not expecting to see my sister and brother here tonight. And everyone looks back at me, speechless that Pastor even knows who they are.

"Have we met?" Kenny asks.

My parents look puzzled as well. I explain quickly. "I assume it's you, Nicole mentioned her brother and sister might be joining. She told me your legal names once, but she keeps referring to your nick names so that's instilled in my head. I hope that's OK."

This satisfies all. Darnell takes the cue and after getting a big kiss from my mom, who isn't satisfied with a hug from her daughter...she just can't help herself, he hugs Trina and Kenny. I shake my dad's hand, but my mom doesn't let me get away with it with her. She pulls me to her and hugs me. She may be feisty but for her, no one is a stranger for long. It feels good to touch her, but I have to stay in character and refrain from hugging her too long. It takes all the strength I have, not to brush my cheek against hers. I miss our phone calls. I told Darnell to call and talk to her at least every other day and to make sure to do it at work so he wouldn't have to talk long, using the excuse, "I'm busy and just want to make sure you're OK." I told him it was either that, or he could expect another pop-up visit. He was happy to oblige; he wants to avoid that at all costs.

It's almost comical to shake hands with my siblings. It's been a couple of months since I've seen either. All of us are spread out in different parts of the city. I see the people at church more than I see them.

My mom cooked smothered pork chops, rice, cabbage, and sweet potatoes. We all fix our plates and sit down for dinner. As we eat, we have some small talk but I'm on edge because they're asking me questions about the church and my background, and why I wanted to be a pastor. I answer most because Darnell had already told me what to expect, but some questions he has to craftfully answer on my behalf when I hesitate. I play like I'm chewing, and he answers things like, "Oh, I think I remember you saying you studied four years."

One question caught me off guard and I actually spit soda out of my mouth. My mom asks, who she thinks is me, "Nicole, are you pregnant?" And I just lose it. My siblings quickly look at my body, you can tell they are rocked by the question too, but I'm the one who reacts.

Darnell calmly says, "No, why would you think that?"

"Kenneth, did you see how much food she had on that plate?" my mom asks my father the rhetorical question. "And I've never seen her eat that fast before. She's eating like a man, with all that meat."

"Leave her alone, you said she was sick. She's just getting her appetite back," Daddy says.

After dinner, I try to save Darnell by helping clean up, but of course my parents don't dare let a guest do any work and they insist I go into the living room with the guys and watch TV. It is a pretty somber experience to be in your parents' home, surrounded by your siblings, and you can't give them the embrace you're accustomed to. But it is neat to actually look at yourself interacting with your family. It's like watching a movie. I wonder if this feels like those out-of-body experiences people say they feel after they flatline or clinically die and their spirit hovers over their physical body but are then resuscitated back to life and can clearly and consistently tell you what people were doing and what was going on all around their lifeless body.

After we leave, we feel it best not to talk in the driveway, but to call each other on the way home, just in case our conversation is overheard.

A little later, after I get to Darnell's house, he calls me again and lets me listen to a voicemail my brother left me. "Hey Nickie, I know he's your pastor and all but there's something wrong with this cat. I can't put my finger on it though. I asked Daddy what he thought, and he said he liked him, that there was something familiar about him, whatever that means. Anyway, I say keep your guards up."

# 20 Nicole

I MEET DARNELL in my condo. I need to pay the rent and there's some things at work I need to show him how to do in person. I also get some more outfits coordinated and ready, so he doesn't have to think about it, he can just grab and go in the mornings. Although from what I see him wear, he doesn't think at all about what he puts on his own body. I'm here for about three hours. I leave, and Darnell locks the door behind me. As I walk down the hall to catch the elevator Terrance steps out!

I can't help it. I grab him and hug him. It's not totally awkward. It's like a man consoling another man, at a funeral or something, or when you see someone you haven't seen for a long time. It seems like forever since I've felt his skin against mine. He smells fresh, like he just finished taking a shower. The hug is too short, and I feel my eyes get misty.

"Man, what's up? Do I know you?"

"Oh, I know you. You're Nicole's boyfriend. Didn't we meet because I never forget a face?" He gives no response. "Sorry, I'm Nicole's pastor." I stretch out my hand, another opportunity to touch him.

He shakes it with skepticism. "No. I've never visited your church."

*Think Nicole, think.* "She has a picture of you on her desk at church. Yes, yes, that's where I've seen you. And she talks about you all the time, you have the most winning record at your law firm. Very impressive."

"So, what are you doing here in Nicole's condo? Preachers make house calls?"

"Of course, we do. And Nicole has missed church, which is very unusual, so I came to check on her."

"She's been sick."

"Yes, I know, which is why I came to check on her."

"So, she lets you come see her but doesn't want me to come see her?"

"Oh, no I didn't see her; she never answered the door. But if you don't mind me waiting to see if she answers for you just to make sure she's okay." I only say this because I just left, so Darnell may naturally open the door without looking through the peephole, assuming it's me, and say something in front of Terrance that can't be explained. I should have said that I did see her, but I'm not good at this and didn't think it through. And if I would have hesitated, he wouldn't believe me either way. *Darnell, please look through the peephole first. If you assume it's me coming back, it's over. He'll know I lied, and he'll assume something is going on.*

Terrance rings the doorbell and immediately knocks on the door. Darnell opens the door while he's talking. "What did you forget?"

"Who were you expecting?" Terrance asks, his voice escalated.

I've showed pastor a picture of Terrance on my phone, so he should recognize him, but just in case, I jump in. "Nicole, I bumped into your boyfriend. I came to check on you. Did the maintenance man just leave, I saw him go down the hallway? Is that who you thought was at the door?" *Take the hint, Pastor!*

"Yes, but he had the wrong condo number."

"OK, I guess you didn't hear me ring the doorbell. I should have knocked like Terrance did."

"No, sorry. I went to the bathroom. Please come in."

Darnell hugs Terrance, an appropriate response for a girlfriend that should be missing her boyfriend. "Don't get too close, I don't want to get you sick, or you Pastor."

"Terrance this is a surprise I was not expecting you...or you Pastor. Why didn't you call?"

"Because I knew you would tell me not to come and I needed to see for myself what was going on." Terrance says.

"Right, what he said." I muster up to sound believable.

I pretend to be concerned and ask my own body if she needs anything. Darnell does not want to be alone with my boyfriend, and I don't want him to either. We haven't gone over enough information about Terrance. I just gave him the basics, because I had no intention of them ever seeing each other, not under these circumstances anyway. But there is a thin line here, if Darnell says yes, he would like something or needs help in any kind of way, Terrance will be offended that his girlfriend is asking her pastor to do something when her boyfriend is right there and can easily do it. Terrance will feel disrespected and threatened. But Darnell does not want me to go.

I have two ideas that can possibly get Terrance to leave and show me more of what he's made of in the process. But first I have to wait for Darnel's answer. Terrance is staring me down, so I can't give Darnell any signs through my facial expressions.

"Thank you, Pastor, but no, I'm fine. I really need both of you to leave so I won't get you sick. And I can get my rest," my body says.

"Don't worry about me, I'll be fine. I'll take care of you. Pastor, thank you for stopping by." Terrance cleverly dismisses me.

"Alright, but Sister Freeman please don't hesitate to call me for anything at all. You're my right-hand man, well woman, and I need to keep you healthy."

"So, you only want her healthy to help you."

"He didn't mean it like that," Darnell says.

Terrance is getting pretentious. My very presence is causing him to get defensive. The second of my ideas to start talking about church business with Terrance's "girlfriend" in the hope Terrance would get bored and leave, is definitely not going to work. It's time for me to go. Darnell is on his own. But I still have to follow through with my first idea, even though now I know Terrance will not budge. I look at them both and say, "Before I go, I want to pray for Sister Nicole's health. Is that alright?" Terrance doesn't respond at all. "Of course, Pastor," Darnell quickly says. I touch my own shoulder like a concerned pastor should, pray and leave. On the way to the parking lot, I pray another prayer, that Darnell can get rid of Terrance soon after I'm gone.

# 21 Darnell

I PULL INTO the parking lot of a tan modern-looking strip center. There are rows of full parking spaces. I don't see an empty space. Ah, I spot white back-up lights and wait. *Thank you, Jesus.* I park the car and brace myself. The black and gold sign on top of the building says, The Beauty Spot, with lettering that match the same name on the door. There's a car insurance place to the left and a Mexican ice cream parlor on the right called La Casa de Helado. I look in the mirror on the visor, wondering if I can somehow make this hair style last, but I know Nicole won't let me keep wearing this pony tail, so I suck it up and flip the visor back up. I see a woman yelling to two little girls whose hands she's holding, and I hope they're not going where I am. *Keep going, keep going...of course not.* If this a prayer, I've been denied. I don't want to be here and definitely don't feel like hearing a parent reprimanding her kids the whole time. "This should be interesting," I say to the empty car.

Although I can't see through the glass door, whoever's on the other side can probably see me sitting here, so I might as well get out now.

I walk into grand central station. Who would have thought all this activity was behind those floor-to-ceiling tinted glass windows? There are at least twenty women in here. I people watch while I constantly look at the time. Stacy, Nicole's beautician, eventually calls me to take her chair. She's young, looks no older than mid-twenties. Her face is made up to perfection, with purple eye shadow and thick eyebrows that seem to be airbrushed on her deep dark-brown skin. She puts a perm on Nicole's head then we go to the shampoo bowl to get it washed out. She adds neutralizer and washes it out, I sit at the bowl with conditioner on my head, then get that washed out. Her phone rings and she sits me back in her chair while she answers it and walks to a back room and closes the door. When she emerges all she says is, "Nicole, girl, I'm sorry I've got to leave. It's an emergency."

"Well, I can't leave like this. I don't know what to do with this." I gesture to my towel-wrapped damp hair. Stacy searches for a solution as her eyes zig and zag to the beauticians and their clients at every station, each at a different stage of getting their hair fixed, and then to the hair dryers to see the number of people under them and add that to her calculation. That must not be feasible because now she's looking across the room at an older lady sweeping up hair and walks over to her. She looks like she's in her fifties, with long loose curls that fall below her shoulders. The lady puts the broom and dustpan up and walks back to her chair. She looks at me and smiles. "Of course, come on Nicole, I'll finish you up." Stacy whisks past me and says "Ms. Rachel's got you. Thank you for understanding." As she reaches the door she looks over her shoulder and shouts, "Thank you, I owe you one."

So, now I'm looking at Ms. Rachel and she's looking at me, like *what in the world did I get myself into*. My eyes must have said the same because she says, "It'll be alright. I'll take good care of you. Stacy told me to give you the usual."

"Wait, I don't think I want the usual." Her eyes widen, and she waits for me to explain. "I just want to do something totally different. How would *you* fix my hair? You know what you don't even need to tell me, it doesn't matter, just fix it however you like." As pretty as her hair looks, I can't go wrong.

"OK then."

She quickly unwraps the towel from my head and gets started like she already knows what she wants to do. Good, I've been here long enough. If Nicole would have told me Stacy would have me waiting over forty-five minutes before she even got started on me, I could have brought my bible. And I probably would've been finished already if she would've kept working on me until I was completely done instead of stopping to roll one lady's hair, then curling another lady's short hair with the smallest set of black curling iron rod's I've ever seen. Wash, stop, get out the chair and sit over there, conditioner, rinse, stop, sit back over there. I close my eyes and let out a long breath. At least at the barbershop, once I'm in the chair I stay until he's through with everything, cutting my hair and trimming my goatee. I notice rows of nail polish on a side table next to Ms. Rachel. I hold out my hands. "And will you do something with these?"

She chuckles. "Nicole, you know I don't do acrylic."

"I just want them off, that's all."

"That I can do. When I put you under the hairdryer, I'll let you soak them in the solution. I'm surprised. What's gotten into you?"

"I'm just doing something different, that's all."

"There's nothing wrong with that."

Ms. Rachel spends the next twenty-five minutes rolling Nicole's hair and leads me to the hair dryer. I sit under this dragon-breathing contraption for over an hour. This is torture. Is this really necessary? It can't be that serious. I know I keep asking her when it's going to be over, but I've got to get up and move around, get me some water or something. I pull up the lid and escape the hot box for a moment. I go to the vending machine and buy a bottle of water. I guzzle it down and stand there for a moment, trying to avoid sitting back in that chair, but I have no recourse, so I slowly walk back to my prison. At least I'm entertained by all the ladies talking nonsense about their plans tonight and showing each other outfits in magazines. *Why are they so loud?* I can't help but hear them, even over the steady hum of this dryer. I shake my head. "Silly women." It just bursts out before I can take it back. I don't realize they hear me at first, but everybody has stopped talking. *How can they possibly hear me with all this noise? Oh no, I need to fix this right now.* "Sorry, that's what my father would call us if he could hear us talking." I clear my throat. "What I mean to say is, a man is not looking for a real woman in a club. Y'all coming here to get your hair done and everything, not to look good on Sunday morning at church but to look good tonight at the club." No one says anything, so I continue. "And a real man doesn't want to see all your stuff. He doesn't want to see all your assets up front. And if you're his woman he certainly doesn't want another man to see what's his." I'm on a roll. "You're spending all this time on your outward appearance, but a real man wants to know will you be a good mother for his children. A man wants to see the authentic you, your true beauty, not the fake stuff you bought to try to trick him, that's false advertisement. If you have to take off your weave or wig, your fake nails, fake eyelashes and set them all on the dresser, he might as well get on the dresser too." I've already started, so I might as well finish. "And why do you buy fake hair and glue it down and then take it out? It's taking out your real hair. A man wants to see a woman's real hair no matter how short it is. I'd rather see a woman's real hair than fake any day." I've said too much. I quickly throw in, "And that is what my father used to tell me verbatim. Haha. My high school drama class came in handy. I sound just like my dad." I throw in another laugh for good measure.

Crickets. I mean not a sound. The only thing to be heard are the hair dryers. *What do I do? Should I run? Are these women going to turn into an angry mob? Say something.* "I took it hard too but when I sat down and really thought about what my dad was trying to teach me, it made sense. And that's why I'm trying to change the way I do things...baby steps." *Did they buy it?*

Finally, some lady who could be the poster child for fake says, "I know how to get a man. I know what they like."

"OK LaQuisha," someone urged.

"You can get one, but can you keep one?" I know I'm bold, but her cockiness sickens me. "And you better be sure of what kind of man you got. A lot of men you're dating don't want *you*; they want what you got, whether it be your money or your body."

Some of the ladies start chiming in. "Girl, what else did your daddy say?"

Oh, I'm a little stunned. I look around the room. They want more. OK, I can do that. "He told me women have the most power. You don't know how beautiful you are, I mean *we* don't know how beautiful we are."

I look at LaQuisha and do my best girlfriend impression. "Girl, if you really want to know what kind of man you have...if you really want to know if he loves you, shut it down. Don't give him any and see how long he stays. And by the way you'll probably get a job sooner if you change your name on your resume."

Oh, too soon. She's giving me that 'stay out of my business look' but she's the one that's putting all her business out there for everyone to hear. "I overheard you earlier saying you're not getting called for interviews. I just thought I'd give you some advice from what I've seen done on my job, that's all." *This is the one good thing that's come out of learning Nicole's job, how to protect yourself from job discrimination, and I want to help anyone I can with it.*

"And what do you do?"

"I work at a staffing agency and we coach people through every stage in the hiring process."

"Go on."

*Whew, OK* "What's your middle name?"

"Shauntanisha."

"And your full name is?"

"LaQuisha Shauntanisha Coleman."

"Just put down Shaun Coleman or L.A. Coleman on your resume. Look, your parents have every right to name you what they want but I'm begging you, don't do that to your children. You're going to limit them. It's all about hiring discrimination. In the corporate world, well any place for that matter, people can find ways to discriminate against you, and your name is one of the first ways they can do it and get away with it. One of the rules companies must adhere to is if you fill out an application and get an interview, then they legally have to keep a record of your resume and notations from the interview for the

EEOC, the Equal Employment Opportunity Commission. But if they see a name they don't like or one that doesn't fit with their culture they just throw it away before you even have the chance to get an interview. They don't even have to keep a record of ever receiving your resume in that case. And people with names that sound white get interviews fifty percent more of the time than people with African-American sounding names."

"That's good to know, thank you. What else did your father say?"

"A lot of men target women with children because they know you probably have a steady job and a place to live since they know you're providing for your kids. And odds are you're either getting child support or some type of government assistance. It doesn't mean they really want to be with you. They may just need a place to lay low for a while until they get themselves together, you know, save up enough money to do something different. In the meantime, they'll let you take care of them."

"You mean use us."

"Yes. And when they're ready to move on, they'll give you an excuse. Either your kids are unruly, or it's not working out, whatever...whatever." I notice the woman with kids pretending not to pay attention but she's quietly considering what I'm saying, so I throw in "And don't think having a baby for a man is going to keep a man. It didn't keep your last two...I'm speaking hypothetically here...Don't get a baby from every man you date. That's insane. Your man should make things easier for you, not harder. His job is to be the priest, protector, and provider of his home. He doesn't automatically start after you get married; he should be doing this now while you're dating. For example, you shouldn't be paying for anything when you go out on a date. That's his responsibility. He's supposed to pursue you not the other way around. The Bible says a man that finds a *wife* finds a good thing. Ladies it's not your job to look, so stop. Start working on yourself and get yourself right. Take care of your kids if you have any; then the right man will find you. Last thing, and I'm done…God is not going to bless you until you stop treating your child's father wrong. Most women are too busy trying to pump him out of more child support money and you won't even let him see his own kid. You're too busy trying to hurt him and you don't even realize you're hurting your own child worse in the process. And the money that you are getting, you're not spending it on your child, but the child will grow up and get you. They'll resent you. And the man you got now isn't going to marry you because he's scared you're going to do the same thing to him. I've done a lot of counseling being a pastor and…I mean, *with* my pastor…Alright I'm gone. Ladies have a good day. Ma'am, how much do I owe you?"

"Ma'am? Nicole, what's going on with you?" Rachel tilts her head. "Ninety-five."

"How much?"

"Ninety-five. Remember, Stacy put a perm on you before she left. I finished styling your hair and your nails." She points to Nicole's newly manicured hands and clear-polished nails, that highlight the natural white of her real fingernails.

I reach inside Nicole's purse and give her the bank card. *A haircut only costs 15 dollars.* "And she comes…I mean, I come every week?"

She shakes her head like I'm playing or something.

"Nicole. You're not even all the way dry yet. What's on your mind?"

"What? Oh, I, I got caught up talking…" I let my voice trail off. I feel like I'm giving truth to what people say about a typical preacher, never knowing when to stop talking. I go sit back under the hair dryer and Rachel adjusts the lid."

Fifty-five minutes later, Rachel frees me from the chair and I go sit back at her area. She's doing all kinds of stuff to Nicole's hair, but I can't see what, since she has my back facing the wall mirror. I look at my watch and just want to leave. I got caught up in the moment and I don't think I've done Nicole any favors with my rhetoric. I probably made her look self-righteous or maybe I'm just second-guessing myself. I close my eyes and pray this is over soon.

I feel the chair turn as Rachel asks, "What do you think?"

I open my eyes. "My God, you're a beautiful woman."

"Go ahead with the positive self-talk. OK. Self-love, that's good Nicole. I'm glad you like it."

My heart is pounding; I feel it in my chest as well as hear it reverberate in my ears. Underneath all the man-made materials she constantly wears, Nicole is breathtaking. I need to pull myself together.

"Oh, yes, you did a wonderful job, really nice. Thank you."

Rachel removes my smock and I get up and nod at her. I don't have any more words to say. I quietly proceed toward the door without a word.

# 22 Nicole

Pastor Darnell told me to arrive at the barber shop for 7am. I'm here and sure enough there are cars already in the parking lot. He told me the barber's name is Rodney, but everyone calls him Red, and his chair would be in the middle. I greet the people inside and acknowledge who must be Red. I'm not sure if he got his nickname from his hair color, which is a natural shade, or his skin color, but the name fits him perfectly. I expected him to be an older man with grey hair but he's probably the same age or younger than I am.

"You running a little late this morning, or do I need to change the batteries on that clock up there?"

"Oh, yes I'm just fifteen minutes late." *Pastor must really be consistent.*

Red apparently has just finished this man's head because he has a fresh haircut and Red is giving him change so I sit in Red's chair.

"Whoa, whoa Pastor, what are you doing?"

"Uh, you're supposed to cut my hair."

I see people looking around at each other; one man drops his head.

Red turns around. "No, Pastor I got four ahead of you."

"What do you mean?"

The barbershop is suddenly silent. I feel the eyes. "I was told to be here for seven. I know I'm a few minutes late, but don't I have an appointment?"

"No. I don't make appointments. Pastor, are you alright?" He grins.

He holds out his hand, gesturing for me to sit in one of the waiting chairs. I can't even look any of the brothers in the eye. Now I just want to hide my face in a magazine, and I quickly scan the room and find none. Great.

Another barber turns on the television and before long, chatter emerges. I play on Pastor's phone for a while, looking at his apps; YouVersion and DailyBible. The bible ones don't surprise me, but Instagram and Facebook do. I didn't know he had time for that. I start browsing and guess I get lost in his phone because the loud talking turns into oohs, and ahhs.

I look toward the TV and see a game being broadcast.

"Oh, rewind it, rewind it," A man in a baseball hat says.

I stand corrected. It's a recording of an earlier game, possibly last night's.

"No, he was down. That wasn't a fumble," another man shouts.

"No, look at his feet. Bad call."

"They should have asked for a replay."

This is interesting. They're really into this.

"Pastor what do you think?"

Oh, one of the men is asking for my opinion, not just another barber, but a patron. That's good. So, Darnell normally comments on stuff like this. That's nice. I always imagined him being stuffy and straight-laced, in other words boring. I pictured him coming in with his Bible and reading the whole time, but he does take his head out of the Bible sometimes, at least when he gets his hair cut. I thought I'd have to teach him how to loosen up and be balanced and have a life outside of church. We'll see, the jury is still out on that.

"I didn't see that part too good. But the man shouldn't hit him that hard. And those uniforms don't even match." Oh, no. I did not just say that. Out of the corner of my eye, I catch one of the barbers fling his wrist down.

"No, I'm straight. Uh, that's just something my sister would say. I guess I miss her. Sorry." I need to be careful, I do sound like a woman. And Pastor doesn't even have a sister, I do. I've got to be careful with what I say. At least I can explain that to mean my sister in Christ, if I need to.

I look out the window and see a couple of women who look like they are in their thirties, with scantily clad clothes on, one with a very short mini skirt, the other with so much cleavage showing, if there would have been under age boys here, I'd have to cover their eyes. I lean back against the chair, curious as to what this room full of men will say or do. I've been subject to catcalls before but not because I dressed provocatively. For me, the attention was unwarranted and unwanted but that may not be the same for all women. Some women like the attention. I'm not one of them. I watch their eyes and brace myself for the impending conversation. The women get closer and closer and walk past the window, seemingly unnoticed. I'm surprised and pleased at the same time. No one says anything. A few eyes looked their way, as did mine, but no comments, no jokes, no nothing. Sometimes nothing is good, especially in this situation. The woman in me wants to ask the men what they think when they see a woman dressed that way, but I don't say anything. I wonder if they feel sorry for them, like I do, or if they are turned off by a woman who shows everything she has. Like my dad always says, 'You leave nothing to the imagination.'

This is taking longer than I imagined. Men's hair is way short. I thought I'd be in and out of here. Red's cut two men's heads since I've sat down. It's already 8:15. By the time he gets to me it will be almost 9 o'clock. I guess I still won't stay as long as pastor will. He may be at the beauty shop all day. I'm kind of glad to get a break from that. We agreed to keep each other's routines, which is about the only normal thing we've got going right now.

Someone's walking up to the door. I recognize that face. He quickly says good morning to everyone and switches into business mode.

"Anybody want some DVD's? I've got some new releases, all high quality. Five dollars each or three for ten."

He normally sells them two for five. "Hey Jerry, what you got?"

Jerry arches his eyebrows, but he walks over to me.

"You normally sell these two for five. You went up?"

He leans back to examine me. "These have always been my prices. And this is the first time you've ever been interested in my catalog."

"Pastor, you know Jerry?" Red asks.

"Uh, yeah, I hear you say his name all the time."

Jerry's not convinced. What, he thinks I'm an undercover officer or something?

As I'm looking through the movie titles, I change my mind. I'm not sure how this would look. Darnell's pretty straight laced, and I don't know how he would feel if I bought some bootleg movies. And these men, I feel their eyes, like they're waiting on me to see what I'm going to do. This won't look good for the pastor's reputation. I don't want to give anyone anything to talk about, so I say, "OK, I was just making conversation. And curious as to what kind of product you have. You have some nice inventory, a lot of new movies I haven't seen yet."

"Yeah, OK." Jerry all but snatched his box from me, somehow relieved I didn't trap him. He quickly says, "Alright, I'll catch y'all next time," and dashes to the exit.

Before the door could close good, someone blurts out, "I was gonna talk about you preacher, buying bootleg," says the man in shorts who just put three of Jerry's movies in his vest pocket.

"Uh, didn't you just buy those from Jerry?" I ask.

"Yeah, but I can do that."

My look demanded an explanation.

"I'm not a preacher."

"What does that have to do with anything?"

"You all got to live to a higher standard."

"If you think it's wrong but you do it, why do you have to hold me to a higher standard?"

"I don't think it's wrong, but that's not what the law says."

"So, you can break the law, but I can't?"

"Hey, you're the one that accepted the call."

"Huh. I turn my head slightly, like it will help me understand his thought processes better."

"Alright Pastor Darnell, you're up," Red summons.

Finally. I leave the man in shorts to his own double-standard thoughts.

"What'll it be this time?"

After two hours I finally get in the chair. The most important thing I was supposed to remember, and it slips my mind. I don't panic though because I wrote it on my hand as a backup. "Taper." I turn my hand back over and manage a little smile at my cleverness. He turns the clippers on and I lock up. I've never had

112

a razor on my head. I learned at an early age that a woman's hair is her glory and covering and should never have a razor put to it. Both my dad and mom instilled that into me and Trina. That's one bible verse we'll always remember. I instinctively turn and lean over to look in the wall-length mirror. I don't know, I guess I want to make sure I'm still in the pastor's body. That is him and not me who will have a razor plowing through his head. I let out a sigh and lean my back against the chair.

"Pastor, you alright? Relax, man. You're stressing."

I almost gasp when the razor starts cutting through my hair. I see it falling to the ground. I feel like I'm getting my scalp massaged. Not bad. He takes about twenty minutes on my head. Then to my surprise he says, "Let me touch up your gray."

"What gray? I mean no. No, leave it."

He hands me a mirror, like I've seen him do with the other men, to approve his work or ask him to fix something. I need to look closely so I don't miss anything. I definitely don't plan on coming back here. I tighten my grip on the handle. "Wow." I touch pastor's face with my free hand. Looking at his reflection this close…he cleans up well, I must say. There is a deep intensity in his eyes I never noticed before. *Ah, there is a small patch of gray hair peeking out the bottom edge of his goatee. Kind of sexy. OK Pastor.*

"Pastor, you good?"

"Hmmm, apparently so. I mean yes, yes. Thank you."

I pay Red and leave before I unintentionally persuade him to make a phone call to check on my well-being. When I get outside I can't help but laugh as I wonder what in the world he may be thinking of my interesting behavior.

# 23 Nicole

PART OF MY job duties at work is to increase sales and drive efficiencies to maximize profit. I can utilize my skills to also help the church. It's time Pastor sees a new perspective on things. I walk into the finance office and see Sis Brenda, the finance secretary waiting for me as I had requested.

"Hello Sister Brenda. Thank you for coming on such short notice."

"No problem at all, Pastor. What can I do for you?"

"I'd like to see a financial report for all our members."

"What exactly do you want, an aggregate, or a percent to prior year assessment?"

"No, I want to see a total of all the donations given by each family for the last three years, separated by category; tithes, offerings, benevolence, love offering, etc."

She looks at me like I have two heads.

"What's wrong?"

"Uh, nothing, just, well, you've never asked for this before and when I've tried to give them to you in the past, you always refused to look at them."

*Oh, he was too busy huh? Well, I'm not.* "I guess I'm turning over a new leaf and I apologize for not taking you seriously."

"Oh, no Pastor, it's not a problem at all. I didn't mean to imply that. I know you appreciate what I do."

"Yes, I certainly do. You're invaluable. How soon can you have them ready?"

"It's just a touch of a few buttons. Do you want it on a flash drive or printed out?"

"Printed."

"OK, then I should be finished in about thirty minutes."

"Great, I can't wait to get started." Our financial program was installed years ago, under Reverend Andrews. I'm the one who compiled a comparison list for each program we were considering, which included capabilities, pros and cons, cost, etc. I'm not sure what features Reverend Andrews ultimately used but he agreed with my program choice. And I know everything this system can and cannot do.

I will use this information to assess our financial condition, hold the members accountable, and strengthen our church. *Lord, since you allowed this to happen, I'm going to take advantage of it and make some changes…much needed changes.* Ms. Brenda hands me the reports. I thank her and put them in my bag. I'll look at them when I get home and figure out what I'll do next.

I make it to Darnell's place and immediately take out the papers. I mull over the information. I consider calling Sis. Brenda to double check if the figures are correct, but sadly I know they are. The combined individual contributions of everyone at the church match up with the grand total income number. It's quite astonishing. I notice right off that a single mother of three gives more than a well-off couple who sport new cars every couple of years. I also see a couple of leaders who are always in the pastor's face, and claim they love this ministry so much, yet they give so little. There's no way they're paying all their tithes, I know what kind of jobs they have and if they aren't making six figures already, they've got to be very close. This is sickening. The next time I see them, I should tell them to put their money where their mouth is. I call Darnell and let him know I'll send communication to the leaders that I'm calling a meeting. It's kind of last minute, but it's necessary.

"Hey Nicole."

"Hi. Real quick, I just want you to know that I'm calling a Leadership Meeting."

"Not only do I have to learn your stuff at work, I have to worry about what you're trying to do with the church. Why don't you just wait it out until things get back to normal?"

"And I have to do the exact thing you're doing. I don't know everything you're doing as me, at my job."

"What's the meeting about?"

"Commitment and…True Leadership."

"What are the specifics?"

"I've got one topic in particular and hashing out the rest in my mind."

He huffs. "A, I don't want you to call a meeting and B, you're not giving me details on what the meeting is about. I feel like I'm losing control of everything."

"Why can't you just trust me?"

"It seems I don't have a choice. You're going to do what you want anyway. But thanks for the heads up."

We hang up and I get out my pad to sketch out an agenda. Then I pray.

# 24 Nicole

NOW THAT I know exactly how I want to approach the meeting, I call Darnell. I'll at least let him know what I'm going to discuss at the meeting tonight, so he won't be caught totally off guard. When he answers, he starts right in. "Nicole, I...there's no way I can finish all this and make it to the meeting tonight."

"I know. That's why I'm usually a few minutes late but the only thing you should have left to do is printing out the stats and leaving your commentary for Gary. And remember, make sure it's in bullet form, he doesn't like paragraphs of information."

"But I still have to do the contract reports."

"Noooo, I told you to give that to Ethan and Uri. They do that. All you're supposed to do is run the reports because they don't have the authorization for that system. Give them the printouts and let them do what they do."

"But they didn't ask for it? If it's their job, why didn't they come to me?"

"Because it's not their butts on the line, it's mine. If you don't give them the information they can't do it. They're helping you out. Why can't you understand that? It's impossible to do everything by yourself. I told you that."

"Why are you upset? Can't it wait until Monday?"

"You just don't get it. I have processes in place to make sure things get done on time. I told you exactly what to do, every day. All you had to do was go down the list and do it exactly the way I told you to."

"Well, I don't think those guys really appreciate you telling them what to do?"

"What? Listen to what you're saying. What exactly did you say to them?"

"This morning, I asked them if they had time, if they would print out the perm reports you had on the list. And they didn't get those to me until the afternoon."

I let his words sink in, analyzing each one, but more importantly what he doesn't say. I sit back in my chair. "You've never asked *me* 'if I have time.' You tell me what you need and when you need it and I find a way to get it done. So why would you ask those men if—" I gasp, the answer is as clear as day. "Pastor Darnell, you have a problem."

"Exactly, that's what I'm trying to tell you."

"No, that's not the problem I'm talking about. At work, there is a chain of command based on levels. My level gives me the authority to delegate certain tasks to others. This is the 21st century and if you have a problem with that, you need to be a hermit. I bet you wouldn't have had a problem giving orders if those men were women."

He doesn't say anything.

"Now, you've got to input all those numbers in the spreadsheet and make sure that report is on Gary's desk first thing Monday morning."

"So what, I've got to work the weekend?"

"You've got a badge to get in the building. Figure it out."

"And you're not going to help me?"

"I helped you by telling you what to do to avoid this. But you didn't listen." I shake my head. "As far as the meeting tonight, make sure you get the food."

"Ah, I forgot about that. Can't you get it?"

"You're the secretary now remember. You've got to do everything I normally do. And make sure it's hot."

"Nicole."

"Bye Darnell." I push the phone down harder than I intend. My mind starts reeling. Is that the reason he's reluctant to take my advice on things concerning the church? What, he expects me to just sit there and not have an opinion? Huh, he's got me messed up. I review my list of changes I will announce tonight. He'll just have to find out with everyone else.

***

I park in the back of the church building, close to the entrance of the fellowship hall. The meeting tonight is for the deacons and leaders of the church, which includes almost everyone that holds a position in the church. As I run the list in my head, the only people who won't be in attendance are the musician and the drummer. And they're the only two people that are on salary besides Pastor Darnell.

I turn the light on and confirm the tables and chairs are already set up in a big rectangle, with the projector in the front. All I need to do now is hook up pastor's laptop to the projector.

I go set my things in his office and go over my notes. I'm just about to leave pastor's office when he walks in and I hardly recognize myself. He has me dressed in one of the outfits I picked out for the week so what I have on looks fabulous but me, myself, I look incredible. You can't help but see my natural beauty. My cheek bones are effortlessly highlighted and nicely sit on their oval canvas. "Wow, you've got me looking so beautiful. You did that!"

"And I have nothing fake on me, well except your purse."

"Ah." After my jaw drops, I smile. He's got a sense of humor. "The real one is so expensive, it's called a handbag, so I won't be upgrading to that anytime soon. Wait, what about my nails?" I get closer and grab my own hand. Simple clear glossy polish highlights the white of my nails. I always thought they looked dull, but a little clear polish does wonders. "They really look nice, and au naturel." I run my fingers through my own hair and admire the shine and bounce it has. I survey my face and see Darnell only put matte foundation on, but it looks like I don't have on any make-up at all. I look refreshing. "Thank you, I look really pretty."

"You're welcome. Are you going to clue me in on what the meeting is about?"

"Sorry, I still have to plug in the laptop and I'm sure mostly everyone's arrived by now. I need to start the meeting on time."

I don't need him to derail me, I need to stay focused and I know if I start telling him the details, he'll start interjecting and second-guessing me and it will just be a distraction to me. I grab the laptop, turn the light off, and shut the door behind us. I put his long legs to good use and walk quickly back. We enter the room. It's a full house and I greet everyone while I plug in the laptop. I sit and scoot the chair closer to the table and accidentally bump my knee on the table ledge trying to cross my legs. A sharp pain shoots through my knee and I grab it. "Ow!" The cry escapes my mouth. I'm still not used to being so big, I do this with my own body all the time without incident.

"Pastor, are you OK?" someone asks.

"Yes, it must be all those years I played basketball."

I direct one of the deacons to pray for the meeting and the meal, before we get started. I massage my knee some more then look at my agenda and sigh. *OK Let's do the easy ones first.*

I say some preliminary things about how pleased I am overall with how the ministry is doing and thank everyone for their hard work and commitment. I talk about how change can be good and share there are a few changes I believe would benefit the ministry. Then I dig right in. "First thing, starting now, I want to perform background checks on anyone who works in the youth department. Let me clarify; anyone 18 and older who works in any capacity with the children. Any questions or comments on that?"

We discuss this won't be a one and done thing, but everyone will be rescreened every couple of years. I explain to the seasoned saints, how schools mandate this for those who volunteer in any capacity and we can learn from the education field. I surprise everyone, even Darnell, when I pull out the results of his background check, which I had done without his knowledge. I pass it around the room, so everyone will fill comfortable with what information is shown on it. I bring home the point that a pastor is subject to adhering to the same expectations he imposes. When it gets to Darnell, he mimics me well by glancing it over. Then he gives a quick nod of approval and a half smile, acknowledging my cleverness.

"Second, everyone in this room holds some type of position within the church. I need all of us to be here at least thirty minutes before each service starts. We need to be an example for the rest of the members, to get here in plenty enough time to prepare what we need to and when we have visitors, they need to always see people in position. I know things happen and there will be times when you won't make it thirty minutes beforehand but that should be the exception, not the rule."

"Third, I need to set a barrier between me and the members. I want five ministers or deacons to be a filter. I haven't decided whether it will be just ministers or if I'll add deacons to this or not. They'll handle the day to day, mundane questions and issues people may have. Each person will have a segment of the alphabet, by last name. For instance, Brother Gladwell might have A through F, Deacon Joe may have G through L."

"Pastor, you may have a back lash on that. You'll have people saying, 'I want to talk to my pastor. So, now he doesn't have time for his members?'" one of the leaders points out.

"I understand that but you in here are going to have to have my back on this. Do you know how many phone calls the pastor gets?" I realize my slip up. "I get. Do you know how much I get?" Blank stares answer me. "I counted it last week. Between phone calls and text messages, I got fifty-two."

"Actually, that's not that bad," someone says.

"That was just on Monday," I state. I let the shock set in, then add, "Saturday, it was seventy-nine."

I see my body's head nod. "Those are the two highest days of the week...probably." Darnell quickly recovers, then adds, "I may have heard Pastor Andrews say that in the past."

"And some members think they're really slick, they're not calling to encourage me for my sermon the next day, they're calling to see if I'm preaching Sunday to decide whether or not they're gonna come to church or stay home." I look at the next topic on my list. "Next, every two years, leaders will change positions."

"You're giving us term limits? This isn't the government," Darnell says. His objection, coming from my body…it's literally something I would say. He's playing me quite well.

"We can make an exception for teachers in the youth department because I know it takes a certain skill set to teach the different age groups and a preschool teacher doesn't necessarily have the patience to teach the high schoolers and vice versa."

"Amen Pastor," one of the teachers remark.

"That's true," another teacher echoes.

"Next, tithing. We all know we're supposed to tithe. I might not can make all our members tithe, but I can for anyone who holds a position in this church, that includes all deacons and leaders. Everyone in this room are in a leadership position and that is tied to responsibility. If you want to have a leadership position you will tithe. If you want to *keep* your leadership position you will tithe. This is a non-negotiable. From now on this will be one of the first requirements listed on every leadership application.

"Let me know your thoughts on this." I look around the table, but I get no takers. "I give my tithes and offering on my pastor's salary, so even I'm not exempt. Take a look at this slide and give me your thoughts." I pull up a bar chart that compares the amount of tithes the leaders have contributed versus regular members. "I don't know how much any of you make but let's look at some figures I pulled up

126

during my research." I proceed to show them the average, median, and the low and high salaries of different professions that are represented in the room and I tie it to what the individual tithe contribution should be. "Now I need each of you to be honest and I ask you to check yourselves. Are you really doing what you're supposed to? God already knows, and you know he does so I'm asking everyone to stop making excuses and do what you're supposed to do." I slowly search the room and make eye contact with as many people as I can. "Without raising your hand, and don't say anything either, I don't want you to perjure yourself, how many of you can truly say you've been obedient to God with your tithes?" I pause. "OK, well, we're all about to see. The next slide I'm about to show you are the tithes of each person in this room over the past year."

"Uh oh."

"Well, wait a minute."

"Can he do that?"

"That's personal."

"Is he serious?"

All types of chatter erupt. And I know I heard somebody curse under their breath. Some people are so scared, I struggle to keep a straight face. I quickly reach for a bottle of water to refocus.

Across the room, I see my body jump straight out of the seat. Darnell has my eyes so big I'm looking like I just saw the devil reincarnate. "Pastor, I need to talk to you for a minute."

"Uh, Nicole, I'm in the middle—" He doesn't wait for permission. He quickly walks out of the room.

I look around the room. "Well, excuse me for a minute. Get seconds or refills, I'll be right back." I turn my papers over, so no one will get a chance to look at my notes, and I go meet Darnell. I'm not quite out of the room when I hear someone whisper, "I think Nicole has something on the pastor; you see how fast he stopped talking. She put him on hush mouth." I act like I don't even hear the comment.

Where did he go? He's not behind the door I just closed. I walk down the hall and still no sign of him, but I see the light on in his office. Before I can get in the door good, he closes it.

"What?! Are you insane? You can't show people's tithes…to other people!"

"Calm down. I'm not going to. I just wanted them to think I was."

"And how did you get the information anyway?"

I give him a look of 'don't play dumb with me.' "The same way you would get the information…if you wanted to. And if you noticed, the same people who were so adamant about having a problem with it, those are the same ones who haven't been tithing. Let's just do a little experiment. Remember who they are. When we get back in there write their names down and you can compare them to the list I'll give you after the meeting."

"This is nonsense. I don't want to know."

"What? This is valuable information. You can see who you're dealing with and who's just giving you lip service. Pastor, you'd be surprised of the people that are always in your face, jockeying for a position, and they don't even love the Lord enough to tithe. Come on, Pastor, stay woke."

"Stay woke?"

I rub my left temple. "It means pay attention, don't be fooled."

"Nicole, why didn't you tell me what you were going to talk about? At least run it by me before you pull this little stunt."

"Oh, like you didn't do at my job when I specifically had everything written step by step, which you ignored?"

"What is this tit for tat? That's not the same and you know it."

"You're right. It's not, because you never told me not to have a meeting."

"Looks like I'm gonna have to apologize to my members and undo some stuff, when I do get back in my body." He squints his eyes shut. "Lord, Jesus, any day now would be great!" I can see the creases around my own eyes and forehead as he speaks. "What else are you about to tell them?"

"First of all, this is not a little stunt. I've been a member here long before you showed up. You think I would do anything to hurt my church? I'm trying to help you out."

"I don't need your help, Nicole."

"Yes, you do. You just don't see it." I grab my own arm to reassure him. "Believe me, I've thought long and hard about these things. And like you said, if you get back in your body—"

"*When, when* I get back in my body…"

I quickly shake my head. "Yes absolutely, *when* you get back, if you see that these changes aren't working, you can just go back to doing what you're doing now."

"Let's get back before they think something they shouldn't." He holds the door open for me.

I point to the door. "That's my job remember."

He grunts.

"Oh, what do we say when we get back in there? You know, how do we explain why we left?" I ask.

"Nothing, you don't owe anyone an explanation. Just keep going where you left off."

I nod. That's the privilege of a pastor.

"And Nicole…no more meetings." He turns and walks ahead of me.

We get back to the fellowship hall and most of everyone has already cleared their trash. Usually more people go for seconds or thirds, but I see some have lost their appetite. I hold in a chuckle and resume my place at the table and turn over my notes. "Let's continue where we left off. Now I ask you, have you been obedient to God?"

"Well pastor, that's between that person and God isn't it?" someone states.

"Right, you don't know everyone's circumstance," another person adds.

"Very interesting comments. But notice I didn't say tithes and offering. I said tithes, which puts all of us on a level playing field. Regardless of income or circumstance, we all are accountable to being obedient to His word of giving ten percent. No matter what.

"I know the statistics that only three to six percent of members in churches across America tithe, and our church is no exception, we teeter a percentage or two above that but what I didn't expect was for those same percentages to include people I have in leadership."

I change the slide. "This is what I was talking about when I said I would show the tithes of everyone in this room, but I meant as an average." I feel the weight of the room lift as people realize their names are not listed. "Look at these two graphs. The one on the left are the percentage of tithes given for the non-leaders, based on average incomes, the one on the right represents the same for everyone in this room; the leaders, teachers, ministers, anyone who holds a position. Now who would have thought the percentages would be almost identical? Do you think that's right? Do you think that's fair to members who look up to you leaders? They expect more out of you. Well, huh, not even more, we're not even up to that yet, because we're not collectively doing the bare minimum. I'm asking you to do what's right. You're already giving at least a tenth of your time to the service of the church, and I'd say your talent too, but your tithe, that's where we're falling short. We've got to do better. That line should be at ten percent at a minimum. I'm not asking for anything more, but God doesn't deserve anything less. Do I have to break down the fact that it takes money for ministry to go forth? You think these lights are on just because Reliant is being generous? No, the church must pay bills just like you do at your own house. All of us want to see a nicely manicured lawn when we drive up on the church ground. It takes money to do that. The lawn man brings his crew out every two weeks without fail. And don't tell me one of you will do it for free. Been there, done that. I need someone reliable. And it's sad to say but sometimes you have to pay someone you don't know, outside the church, in order for them to take the job serious. Think about all the services you use at your own house, water, gas, maintenance to the building, the church vans, supplies, food. It all takes money."

I get many head nods and affirming comments, even from Pastor Darnell. "I reiterate, if you're going to be a leader in this church, you must tithe. So, in order to facilitate that, I want to see your tax return for the previous year. I need both your tax return and your W2's to make sure they match because after this you married couples may try and file separately, so your wife or your husband's income won't be included in the household income I look at. Then you may say that's all you've made, which could really be just half of your household. And remember, your tithes need to line up with the gross income, not the net.

"You're kidding right?" Pastor asks.

"No, Nicole, I'm serious."

"But what if your wife goes to another church?" one of the teachers asks.

"Then you've got bigger problems than tithing. You're not on one accord. You should be a member at one church. It doesn't have to be this one. Pick the one that best suits your family. That should be your first priority."

"And what if we don't show our tax returns?"

"Then you don't want to be a leader or hold a position in this church." I look around the room. "Brothers and sisters, a leader should be held to a higher standard. Am I asking you to do something outlandish? No, you should be paying your tithes anyway. That's a basic requirement of being a Christian, and one of the first acts of faith. Now, as a leader, you have more responsibility. And providing these documents is now one of those responsibilities that I expect everyone in leadership to abide by from now on. If anyone new joins our church and wants to be a leader there will already be an established protocol and be part of the prerequisites when they apply for a position."

I look at my watch.

"And let's try to keep our meetings to no more than one hour so that we all will be respectful of each other's time. I think we'll all be more efficient to complete the business we have set out to do whenever any of us holds a meeting for any auxiliary. Start on time and stick to the agenda but allow time at the end, after you officially adjourn the meeting, for any other one-off questions you didn't get to. So, if we are to adhere to that, we've got about five minutes if anyone has any questions or comments. And of course, we can go over the time, I know I've introduced a lot, but I want us all to start being more conscious of how we structure meetings to account for everyone's other commitments." No one says a word. I look around the room at lowered heads or eyes that roam everywhere except to look at me. "Well then, let's wrap up this meeting. Deacon Joe, will you lead us in prayer?"

He nods once and begins. "Oh, Heavenly most gracious father, be with the man of God as he tries to make us better people, better Christians, and a better church. Let us recognize the spirit in which he's giving us these new directives. Let us continue to pray for you to lead and guide him, so that he can in turn impart your wisdom. Even if we don't understand it all, let us respect the office that our pastor holds and obey him as unto the Lord, not with grumbling or lip service, but in unity of heart. In Jesus' name we pray, Amen."

"Amen," we all collectively respond.

I watch my body jump up. "Well, that's a lot for one night. I...I'll clean up so you can all go ahead and enjoy the rest of your night."

Although a few still had to put their own trash away, it doesn't take long for everyone to pile out. I leave the fellowship hall and go to the pastor's office to put the papers away, get my things, and use the bathroom before I leave.

When I emerge from the bathroom, he's waiting for me. "Did you make sure everyone is gone?" I ask.

"Nicole. What are you doing? Tax returns? Almost all the roles in this church are voluntary. The only ones I have on staff are the musicians. Since I'm paying them, I can expect certain things and lay down expectations but everyone else is doing this on their own time, out of the goodness of their heart. They're not getting any money, they're just doing it out of service to God. Now, point well taken on the distinction of tithes between leaders and non-leaders but if you set an expectation you've got to have faith in the people you're leading, that they'll do what you ask."

"Haven't you heard the term, Trust but Verify?"

"You can't lead with demands."

"So now that I set up some expectations you have a problem with it."

He shakes his head. "Demanding tax returns is totally different. You just can't do that."

"Yes, I can, *you* can. A pastor can set up any rules they want. What we've been doing is not working, so why not try something else?"

He bites hard on his bottom lip then turns and slams the door behind him.

I jump. The force causes one of his plaques to fall off the wall. I catch my breath. I've never seen him like this. I hesitate, standing still, in case he returns. After moments pass, I make up my mind; I'm not going to pick it up. He's the one that can't control his anger. I lift my head and go back to what I was doing.

# 25 Darnell

NICOLE AND I sit down for lunch and without thinking about it, I do what a gentleman does and pull her chair out and she says thank you. The only problem is if anyone is paying attention, they see a woman pull out a chair for a man. But how do you erase over thirty years of good manners and upbringing? I immediately regret my decision, but people have seen worse in this city, and most, if they even notice, may shrug it off to some woman's equal-opportunity shenanigan. But, I didn't count on an elderly couple noticing. An old woman at the adjacent table looks on in disbelief and states, "What is the world coming to? Lord, I've got to go. Check please."

"Let's pay it up front," her male companion offers.

"Oh, no Ma'am, we're doing role reversal. She's treating me the way she wants to be treated," Nicole explains with her sharp wit.

"Yes, Ma'am, our counselor suggested it. It's good for therapy," I add.

"Marriage counselor?" The lady glanced at my...Nicole's bare ring finger.

Nicole noticed. "Well, I know we're not married yet, but yes."

"Oh, so I do to him what I want him to do to me." She extends her arm and squeezes her husband's butt. That's who I assume it is, based on their matching rings.

"Whoa, look at what you've started. But I don't mind." He winks.

I look at Nicole smile and drop her head. I don't think I've ever seen a man blush. And I really didn't think I was capable of it. This is just weird.

I'm hungry but Nicole immediately pulls out her laptop and starts to drill me on the presentation. We've already gone over this ad nauseam. I can think clearer with a full stomach.

"Darnell, this is very important. You need to know this backward and forward. Be ready for any questions that may come up. If he asks you which office has the lowest productivity, you've got to be able to revert back to the correct graph and know your numbers. If you get stuck, know where to find the data quickly. You need to know the percentage of temporary and permanent placements, with temporary split out between contract and contract-to-hire, revenue and contract margins, and give the reasons for the biggest declines at our top clients."

I hear everything she's saying, and I've studied and practiced so I know it will all work out. And if I get stuck, like she said, I have the notes.

"Nicole, I've got it. But I won't be able to think on an empty stomach. Let's order."

She throws her hands up, just like a woman does. I give her the look, to chill, she's making me look some type of way.

"OK Darnell. This is the big opportunity I've been looking for. This can make or break my chance of a promotion. I've just got to trust you."

"Exactly. Trust me." I say this and for a split second, wonder if I'm being hypocritical because I didn't trust her at the church leadership meeting on one change she was trying to make. I understood everything else but asking to see leaders' tax returns and W2's never crossed my mind. And I can't see myself allowing it. I've heard pastors implementing some outlandish rules in churches they serve, and I don't want to be part of that in any way.

# 26 Darnell

WE'RE IN THE middle of another learning session about her job and when we take a break Nicole drops the bomb on me. With a serious face she says, "I want to do the sermon this Sunday."

"Why?" I ask.

"I think it would be neat, uh, and to impart wisdom, from my perspective. Besides, I've always been curious to know how it feels to stand behind the pulpit. We never could get close to the pulpit as a child. Adults back then considered it holy ground. The church I grew up in had the pulpit area in the middle of the stage but the pews the clergy sat in were nestled in what we called the pit because the area was lower than the rest of the stage. The men had to walk two steps down to get to their seats. The entire choir stand wrapped around it on three sides. We little kids had to walk past the pulpit to get to the front and say our Easter speeches. The thought of me veering from that small pathway between the first choir row and

139

the pit by accidentally stepping my toe beyond the threshold and into the hallowed ground had me so scared, I thought I'd be struck by lightning."

The sincerity of her face doesn't match her trifling answer, so I say plainly, "I don't think that's a good idea."

"What, you don't think a woman can do it?"

"It's not that. Nicole, it's not an easy thing to do. There's a difference in speaking and delivering a sermon. I may make it look easy but it's more than just talking, you have to be anointed to do this."

"I have some things I want to talk about."

"You can't just preach what you want to. And you definitely can't go up there with an agenda. If you want to reprimand someone, the pulpit is not the place to do it. You need to have a private meeting for that."

"No, I'm not going to do any of that. I'll have a real biblically-based message. How hard can it be? All I have to do is give three points and a close, almost like a sales presentation."

"Yeah, if you're a visiting minister, you can shout the congregation and do a feel-good message, pick up your honorarium and go home, but a pastor has to know the pulse of the congregation and hear 'what thus says the Lord.' He gives me most of my messages, and sometimes he may give it to me the morning of, or change it right before I'm about to leave my office and go into the sanctuary, and I have to table what I had prepared and say what he tells me at that moment. You've got to be sensitive to the Holy Spirit."

"All I have to do is talk about prosperity, blessings, or coming into your season."

I shake my head. "I know some preachers slop their congregation but you all aren't pigs, you're my sheep."

"I didn't mean it like that. I just meant, I'll preach on something safe. I'll pray about the topic and if He tells me something else, I'll listen and change it too. Besides, you don't want people wandering what's going on with you not giving your sermons. That's not like you at all."

"Nicole, I said you have to be anointed to do this. And anointing comes by spending time with God or overcoming trials."

"Pastor, you're making a lot of assumptions. I do spend time with Him. I may not spend as much time as you do but I'm still anointed. And you don't know what I've been through. As a Christian, I'm not supposed to look like what I've been through anyway, right?"

"OK, OK. I'll give you that. Look, I need to know specifically what you want to talk about. Give me an outline and I'll think about it."

"That's all I ask."

"Nicole, you were right about some of the women."

"Uh, huh," she smiles. "Just keep your eyes and ears open, I'm sure you'll learn more than you want to, but exactly what you need to. OK, listen." She shrugs the topic off. "I've been doing a lot of research and I want to run a couple things by you."

There's no need to say anything, she's going to keep talking anyway.

"I know this is a bit unorthodox, but some churches do this. What are your thoughts on having non-tithers sit in the back and reserve the best seats for the ones who tithe?"

I look at her for a long time. What has she become? And what is she thinking? I calmly say "No, absolutely not."

"OK, what about this?"

She's offering up another "solution" like it's a consolation prize. "Anyone who you have on payroll, what do you think about, automatically taking the tithes straight from their paycheck? Again, there are churches that do that."

I close my eyes. "No to that one too, Nicole. I'm not going to take money from someone?"

"I don't see what the problem is."

I don't know why I'm about to explain this to her, but I do. "Take the musician and the drummer. They both get a salary. I pay them once a month, and I give it to them before the month begins."

"Before they've even done the work?"

"Yes."

"But what if—"

I cut her off. I already know what she's thinking. "That's not my problem. If they run off with the money and don't fulfil their end of the bargain, that's on them. God will take care of it."

She remains quiet, so I keep talking. "The musician and the drummer are in two different circumstances. The musician isn't a member of our church, so he's not obligated to give his tithes to this church, he has a church of his own where he's a member."

"What about an offering then?"

"If he wants to give one, but he doesn't have to, and I'm not going to guilt him into doing so. He provides a service and I pay him, he doesn't owe me anything else."

"OK, what about the drummer then?"

"Yes, he's a member but I've got to trust that he'll do the right thing and pay his tithes, not because he wants to please me, but because he loves God. You can set the expectations for people to give, Nicole, but you can't just mandate everything; God doesn't even do that. Sure, he sets up rules but I'm not God. And you've got to have God's heart to serve God's people. A pastor is a servant, not a ruler."

"Well, I think you can serve and still hold people accountable for what they're supposed to do. What about everything you do to give to everyone else? They need to do their part. How are you going to have some people giving and not others? If that's the case, the contributions in the church will never increase to the level they're supposed to be."

"That's not my problem. I've taught about tithes and offerings and we have a whole section on it in the New Members Orientation class, so everyone knows what they should do. I teach them the word like I'm supposed to do, and I let God take care of the rest. They are his people before they're mine. So, they're not going against me, their being disobedient to Him. Besides, God supplies my need with the people that do give.

"But it seems like you're giving more to the people who don't give back to you. I've seen the pastor's love offering. And only a handful of people consistently give you something. And it amazes me that the people who take up your time the most, are the same ones who give the least, if at all."

"And they manifest my value to themselves with their giving or lack thereof. Some people are takers, and that's all they do, and they'll never be satisfied or blessed with that mindset. They ultimately have to answer to God for that, not me. And that's okay. I just do my part and trust God to provide for me. The people that bless me are blessed in return. The people that don't bless me, they miss out on their own blessing, but I don't miss out. God still continues to provide for me, even if it's through other avenues. It's not a cliché, I say this all the time: God will give a blessing to who he can get a blessing through. I've just got to make sure that my heart is right. But human nature takes over when I can see with my natural eye who does and who does not take the time to give to me personally through a love offering, let alone tithes and offering. And it's important for a pastor to be impartial, which is why I don't want to see some things even though I have the right to do so.

"OK, I understand." She looks down and I hope I've gotten through to her.

# 27 Nicole

I'M GOING OVER the sermon outline Pastor approved.
It's about faith. He said he was impressed with the
points I have and the biblical examples I included.
Earlier, when I practiced speaking it in front of him,
it's like his body naturally took over. I sounded just
like him, with my voice inflections…I even had the
same mannerisms.

This phone keeps ringing. I sigh and look in the
direction of the distraction. I've been ignoring it
because church members keep calling to either
complain about something or for me to fix their
problem. This is too much pressure for anyone. I
throw my hands up. "I guess I'll take a break and
listen to their messages," I say to an empty room.

I listen to the voicemails and after returning three
callers, I call it quits. I almost want to throw the
phone up against the wall. This is ridiculous. The first
caller has issues with her so-called grown children. I
already know the issues because I've overheard her
complain on more than one occasion about

repeatedly having to come to their rescue. I listen without interrupting because I am imitating the pastor. I want to be as compassionate as I've seen him be and I don't know if pastor has heard her issues before, but when she stops talking, I get straight to the point. In an even-keel tone I simply say, "They're twenty-five and twenty-two years old, when are you gonna cut the umbilical cord?" She's quiet for a long time, no doubt processing my shocker of a question, so I simply say goodnight and hang up.

The second call is a man who's angry because his wife isn't giving him any sex. I know his wife and she's a hard worker, outside and inside of their home but her husband acts like he's a king and expects her to wait on him hand and foot. He doesn't cook or clean either. I sat in on an evening marriage class once, when they invited single people who had a desire to be married. I don't know what effect they thought it would have on us singles, maybe to emphasize the fact that marriage is not easy, or to deter us from marrying the wrong person. I just remember I wanted to shake some sense into this egotistic brother, and I felt so sorry for his wife. You could see the unhappiness in her face.

So when he calls, I'm tickled pink. Me currently as a man, I can tell him, what a woman can't, since his pride won't receive it. I go all in on him. I say, "Man she's tired. You come home and she's been dealing with those bad kids of yours and trying to keep the house clean after a full day's work at her own job and all you do is go straight to the TV and zone out. A king takes care of his queen first. You haven't given her any attention and now you want to turn her on and off like a car and ride her to death. Get real. Take care of your wife and she'll take care of you, but it's hard for a woman to meet your needs when you aren't considerate enough to meet hers. Stop being selfish and man-up. Why don't you take the load off her and stop thinking about yourself?"

"I…I never thought about it like that Pastor. Uh, OK. I'll do something."

"Good night," I say and immediately hang up. I'm not playing with anyone now. And I hope they spread the word. Maybe they'll stop blowing the pastor's phone up.

The last call I take is from Sister Mildred, the church critic. She always has something negative to say. No matter what goes on, she will find something wrong in the service. We can have fifty people give their life to Christ during service, but she'll say the music was too loud. I have a short fuse for people like that. She says the church programs for last week's service were tacky because it had three misspelled words in it. She threw in what pastor normally says, but with sarcasm, "And you know we need to do things with the spirit of excellence."

I agree with this mantra, but she nitpicks at everything. She's one of those people who are never satisfied. I believe when you have people with this attitude, it means they don't have anything to do. They're so idle, they can see flaws in everything. But if they were busy helping the church function, they wouldn't have time to criticize. So, I say, "Well then you take over the programs and be the editor."

"Well pastor, I don't have time for that," she counters.

"You're already doing the job anyway, spending all that time looking over it. And you're so good at it. We need people like you. Plus, you'll save a lot of time because you won't have to call me about it, you'd already be done fixing it, before it goes to print, which I'm sure will save you a lot of frustration." I know she can hear the sarcasm in my voice but at this point, I really don't care. She understands exactly what I mean. She initiates the end of the call and I smile after she hangs up.

"That's three less people I'll have to hear from in a while," I say aloud.

Pastor Darnell calls me, and I explain to him the three callers' issues and ask, "Is this what you go through every single Saturday? After addressing it at the meeting I thought the word would get around and you'd get less calls."

My voice chuckles. It sounds like I'm listening to myself on a recorder. "I wish it were just on Saturdays," he says, "You get used to it. I get some dry spells and then there are some days when it's constant. I mean like a dripping water faucet."

I shake my head. "I wouldn't be able to do that on a regular basis."

"You saved the voicemails, right? You can play them for me and I'll craft a response, so you can return the calls. If they don't answer that's even better so you can leave a message on their voicemails."

"Oh, that won't be necessary."

"Nicole, I like to respond to my members as soon as possible."

"Oh, you did."

"What do you mean?"

"I called them all back."

"You what? What did you say?"

"You probably don't want to know, but I handled it like a pastor should, I mean would."

I can tell by his silence, he doesn't know what to think. "Don't worry. I handled it," I assure him.

"That's what I'm afraid of."

"I didn't pacify them, but I told them what they needed to hear." He is dead silent. "Come on, I'm trusting you every day to talk to my coworkers and my boss and do my job. Surely you can trust me to handle a few insignificant matters concerning our brothers and sisters in Christ."

"OK Nicole; you're right."

"Then I'll see you tomorrow morning."

"Yes, get plenty of sleep so you can be there in plenty of time."

"I will, good night."

I made sure to get his final confirmation that I can deliver the sermon tomorrow, before I brought up the calls, just to make sure nothing would reverse his decision. I look over my notes again, but my thoughts are being overtaken with the phone conversations. Why are people calling him with these matters? More importantly, why does he let them? I stand and walk around. I feel an unsettling. *Wait, I remember Pastor saying the Holy Spirit often gives him something else to talk about. Maybe He allowed me to experience those calls for a reason.* I dash back to my notes, look at them again, then turn them face down and tuck them into a folder. *I think maybe the Lord has a more pressing issue he wants me to address.* I pull out my pen and start frantically writing down all the thoughts flooding in my head. This may take me a couple hours to organize but I think this is very timely. And I don't think I'm going to share this with the pastor; he'll have to hear it at the same time everyone else will. I doubt I have the nerve to say it twice anyway. Not every message from God is a feel-good message. It's OK to shake things up right? Of course, He gave this to me anyway. There's no way I'd have the guts to do this on my own.

I spend the next few hours refining the message, then I put my pen down. "Lord, this may not go over well. If this isn't from you, you need to let me know, otherwise, this is what I'm talking about in the morning. Lord, I hope the congregation *and* the pastor are receptive."

# 28 Darnell

SUNDAY MORNING IS finally here and I'm a little nervous having Nicole preach this morning. Even though I know what she's preaching about, I've got to sit there and watch my own body preach. I want to give her some space, so I don't go straight into my office. I walk around the outside of the church for a minute and just observe. I hear a couple of ladies talking. Now that I have this unique opportunity to hear women's conversations up close, I am intrigued to hear what they're talking about. It's nice to hear praise and words of encouragement about your ministry and staff or just hear someone lift their fellow parishioner's spirit as we go through life together. I get closer and their muffled voices are now clear, and I quickly surmise they're not talking about godly inspiration at all, but carnal flesh. I'm used to hearing men talk about women; I've heard it all my life, all through middle school and up into college, even as a sales professional. Some conversations I've heard were good and some bad but when people know I'm a preacher they monitor what they say. Even those with good intentions filter their speech and are reluctant to talk around a pastor at all for fear they'll be judged for one thing or another, either not having enough faith about some issue or because a person even allowed themselves to be in certain situations, so I look forward to experiencing what people talk about amongst themselves, when they know they are out of earshot of the pastor. When I'm around people who have no idea who I am, I get to watch and listen to them in all their authenticity. It's eye-opening, what are on and in people's hearts and minds.

I sit on the bench next to them and start fiddling with the clasp on Nicole's shoes to make myself look busy and mask the fact that I'm eavesdropping. My eyes open wider with every word they utter. They're not even filtering their speech around me. You would think they'd change the subject, but they are unscathed by another woman's presence. They're talking about a man, and how much they want him, want to get with him, and all the things they want to do with him. They're really letting out their dirty laundry. It's obvious this is not their first conversation about him. I'm intrigued but I sit up slowly pretending like I'm not listening. I follow their gaze to see which one of the brothers at the church has got them all riled up. I survey the pack of brothers next to the door and wonder which one they are referring to.

They quickly turn to each other. The lady in the hat says she just wants one night with him just to see how it feels to sleep with a preacher. OK that eliminates two men. Then she asks the woman with all the noisy jewelry on, "I wander what kind of sounds he'll make and how he would be thinking of me as he's sitting in the pulpit." *Lord, have mercy.* The noisy jewelry lady says, "I just want to see if he can practice what he preaches and flee temptation." So, they're preying on my preachers. This is too much.

Two of the three ministers in the huddle are married so even if they're talking about the single one, what they're doing is dead wrong. Preachers have enough to worry about with the everyday added pressures and responsibilities of the heavy weight of the call. I hold them to a higher standard as I help them build their study muscles and challenge them to spend more quality time with the Father, so they will stay anointed and overcome temptation of every kind. It's important for them to stay in the perfect will of God. To hear these women strategize for their demise is incredible. Their thoughts are immoral. I shake my head. This can't be real.

A little of my mother comes out before I know it. "Oooh, you are some scandalous winches." Maybe I shouldn't have said it but right now I feel like Jesus did when he called the religious leaders Vipers when he spoke of their heart. For the mouth speaks out of that which fills the heart. The 34th verse of Matthew 12 just naturally comes to my memory. Words do reveal character.

The hat lady leans over to me and whispers, "Sounds like someone's upset because he's not showing them any interest."

"I have a man." I quickly whip back what I've heard Nicole say.

"You'd better keep him too because if Pastor Darnell wanted you, he would have asked you out by now, so he's clearly not interested."

They're talking about me! My Lord. I know there are some good loving Christian women here, so why is the Lord allowing me to see these Jezebels? I catch myself because I want to bang her head into the wall, maybe it will cast the demon out of her. I jump up instead and stare straight into her eyes. *The Lord rebuke you,* I say in my mind. She recoils like she sees a ghost and I leave without a word.

I make it inside the church. I briskly walk toward my office but shock smacks me in the face and locks up my joints. *Oh, no. Not today!* I turn into a statue and it takes me a few moments to even know what to do or how to act. My thoughts aren't coming fast enough. I try and blink reality away. Standing less than ten feet away are my mother and father.

# 29 Nicole

I GET HERE early and pray. I open the folder and look at both sermon notes laying before me, a faith-filled message on the left and what may prove to be an unpopular message on the right; of which could raise some eyebrows in the congregation and get me in hot water with the pastor. I feel like I'm the one who's been given the ultimate choice between two extremes, do I step through the red door or the blue one? I was so sure last night when it came to me but I'm not sure anymore. "Lord is this you or me?" I get up and walk around the pastor's office. I see the plaques on the wall; Master of Divinity from Houston Baptist University and Bachelor's in Social Work from Clark Atlanta University, and a vertical plaque on his table that commemorates him as distinguished alumni. I fall on the couch to think. Wait, what is that? Something shiny, half hidden behind the bottom of the cabinet. I walk to go pick it up. As I lodge it out, I remember it must be the plaque that fell the day Pastor had his conniption fit. I stare at it. It's the Serenity Prayer, its words engraved in gold on a black background. I don't remember the last time I've read it, so I read it now. I ponder on the last words, 'and the wisdom to know the difference.' *Lord, is this a sign?*

I wait. I listen. But I don't hear anything. No inner voice, nothing tugging on my spirit, not even a still small voice or a simple utterance, or whisper.

I leave to get some fresh air. Maybe a quick change of scenery is enough to get my thoughts together. I make a trek around the building and briefly exchange pleasantries with some brothers huddled in front of the church entrance. Although I've waved and smiled at a few parishioners as they've called the pastor's name, I'm so focused on my inner thoughts, I don't remember who I've spoken to, or if my words were even intelligible.

I make my way back to the office and close the door like I'm getting ready to stay hunkered down in a snowstorm. "Who am I kidding? I can't do this." I say to myself.

A frantic knock interrupts my thoughts. Before I can even reply to the noise, the doorknob turns and I turn around to face Darnell to admit my defeat. I barely let him close the door before I bombard him.

"I've had second thoughts. I can't do this."

"Yes, you can."

"No, you should stand up and talk."

"Uh...," I hear my own voice stammer as I watch my own body. Darnell waves his hands up and down referring to his foreign shell. "I'm in your body. I can't just walk into the pulpit."

"No, but you can stand at the podium as me and talk about…about…the Proverbs 31 Woman. Yeah, that will work."

"Maybe next time. Lord, I hope there won't be a next time." He rushes close to me and whispers, like there's someone in the room who can overhear. "You have to preach today."

"Why?"

"My parents and my brother are here."

"What?" I say, louder than I intend to. "Why didn't you tell me? Why are they here?"

"I didn't know. They call themselves wanting to surprise me I guess. So, you've got to preach. They didn't come to hear anyone else, they came to hear me."

My heart starts thumping. "How will I know which ones they are? I don't remember what they look like."

"I'll make sure to sit beside them. Where's my phone?"

I point to his desk.

He grabs it and returns to where I am. The shock of it all has my feet plastered to the floor. "Here. Here they all are, it's one of the last pictures we took together at their house…Kevin and Glenda and my brother's name is David." He points to each.

"Why do I need to know your parents' names? You don't call them that do you?"

"Right. Dad and Mother."

"Mother? Oh, you sound so uppity. You sure this is gonna work?"

"We don't have a choice. It has too."

"How are you gonna sit with them, you don't even...I don't even know them."

"I'll figure it out. Oh, and she's wearing a red dress, and my dad has a black suit with a red tie."

I watch my body turn to leave. "Wait, what about your brother?"

"He looks just like me you can't miss him." He tilts his head down. "I think he's wearing dark blue but trust me, you'll know. And make sure you act surprised."

Pastor leaves me to contend with my thoughts. Now I have this monkey-wrench to deal with. I have enough on my mind as it is.

I hear the keyboard playing the intro to the opening song. No doubt the seats in the sanctuary are about three quarters full by now. The choir's singing is a backdrop to my prayer. I hope I can deliver a message as good as they sound. After I finish praying, I've made up my mind. I take out the sermon notes from the folder, then I hear pastor's voice in my head about the Holy Spirit changing his topics even as he would leave his office. I don't want to take any chances, so I put the notes back and decide to take the whole folder with me, just in case.

I pray again, with my hand on the doorknob. It's now or never. I take a deep breath and walk into the sanctuary. I stand along the wall and glance over the sea of faces, looking for my own. I see my body seated but it seems like everyone in the congregation is wearing red or black today. And where is his brother? There's no one sitting next to my body that looks like the pastor. *Come on Pastor, look up. Is it the couple on your left, or right?* I've got to go sit down, this looks odd, me just standing here.

The applause of the congregation, for the choir's finished song starts me into motion. I walk up the side stairs and sit, trying my best to look studious as I zero in on where Pastor is. My body stands up and Pastor waves his hands over the heads of two people sitting in front of him. *Oh, there they are. Smile, look surprised. But where is…?* As if on cue, a man that could almost pass for his twin whispers to a man sitting on the end of the row, who gets up to let him pass through. *Repeat; smile and look surprised.*

As the choir ends their third number, I am at peace and ready. I open the folder beside me and take out the message from the right pocket. Something comes over me and I feel fearless. I tune out the announcements as I glance through my notes and say another prayer as the offering basket is passed around. The time has come. I approach the podium.

"Church, you look good this morning. I'm especially glad to be able to come before you this morning because my family has surprised me today with a visit."

Applause and chatter follow. "All the way from Atlanta, Georgia, my parents and my older brother David. You sure did get me this time."

160

They laugh and wave as people around them vie for their attention to offer their well wishes. Do I complement them on how they look? I don't know what Darnell would do in this situation because I've never seen him do it. Since I don't know them, I really can't say too much, and I don't want to say the wrong thing, so I waste no time getting to the message. I'm not even going to think about it too much. I just want to plow through and get it over with.

"Please turn your bibles with me to Exodus, chapter 18 verses 13 through 24. I want to concentrate on two key verses, verses 17 and 18. And the King James version reads, 'And Moses' father in law said unto him, The thing that thou doest is not good. Thou wilt surely wear away, both thou, and this people that is with thee: for this thing is too heavy for thee; thou art not able to perform it thyself alone.' My sermon for today, "Lord, deliver my pastor...from me."

"Alright Pastor."

"OK OK."

Intriguing comments of curiosity trickle in from around the room.

"I need to share some things with you all. I had to wait until after offering was taken up, because well, I know you. If you don't like what I'm about to say you may not give this morning. And I don't want you to miss your blessing, so I waited," I say lightheartedly. "But no, you wouldn't do that, not this church, maybe the church down the street." I get a few laughs. I'm beginning to flow. Those words aren't even in my notes. Darnell is looking at me like 'what is she doing.' I'm trying to avoid his gaze.

I hone in on the weariness Moses experienced dealing with the people's problems all day and night and how his father-in-law Jethro suggested a solution and how later God gave Moses a better solution, to add a buffer between the people and himself, so Moses was freed up to do the work God had called him to do. I focus solely on the story of Moses and we read through some more scriptures as I hit the points I want to emphasize about him missing the Promise Land because he allowed the people to frustrate him when he chose to strike the rock instead of speak to it as God had commanded.

"Listen, I know this may be a shock to you, but I'm human to. I have feelings too. I'm busy too. I've heard some of you say things like, 'it doesn't take all that, and I've got other things to do besides come to church; my life don't revolve around the pastor and the church,'…and this may surprise you, but my life doesn't revolve around you either. So, don't call me after 5pm. Oh, now I'm wrong. Everybody wants a 24-hour pastor, but you don't want to be a 24-hour member. I can't even get half of you jokers to show up on time; that means before church starts. You may or may not come for Wednesday night Bible study and Lord don't let it rain or be too cold outside. It really would be two or three gathered and He in the midst." The laughter means they hear me, and they understand. "And when you call me with a problem, you better already have some possible solutions. I don't have time for all this foolishness. I got a life too. Y'all ain't gonna kill me."

I notice Darnell's mom raise an eyebrow and share a glance with her husband. Darnell has my head tilted down but I can see my eyes shifting all around trying to see how others in his congregation are responding. As some in the congregation say amen, others applaud ferociously. I can't help but look around as well. The saints are really on board with this, urging me on. I'm encouraged by this. I then look closer and further in the corners and towards the back of the church and spot the usual suspects who make a habit of calling the pastor. I remember making note of their call and text histories. They have scowls plastered on their faces, loathing dripping from their pores. It's funny to me how pathetic they look and the nerve of them to be upset. I look at my body again, sitting straight up now, my own face glaring back at me. Pastor slowly smiles and mouths "thank you."

# 30 Darnell

I CAN'T BELIEVE I'm really doing this. Nicole practically begged me, no scratch that, she *flat out* begged me; tugging and pulling on me until I said yes. I guess, if the shoe was on the other foot, I'd want her to do the same for me. And after the incredible job Nicole did Sunday with the sermon, I guess I owe her one. So, I acquiesced. Not only did she bring home a sermon that could have went south quickly, she did it with humor and tact. The congregation could have taken the message either way, but she pulled it off masterfully. She even held it together with my family. I think I was more nervous than she was. After Sunday lunch, I relaxed when my parents and David apologized for not being able to stay longer because he had to get back to work the next day. That was an instant relief.

Now, I'm sitting in the passenger seat telling myself, *you fool, you fool, you fool.* I agreed to go to the Rockets' game with this man, Nicole's beau. So he won't try anything funny, I already told him on the phone that my throat hurts and I'm not feeling the best. That's what Nicole and I came up with, so he won't try to kiss me. Just the thought of it makes me want to throw up. The lie is for his own protection, otherwise he would be going home with a broken nose.

"Nicole, are you alright?"

I guess I made the gesture for real. I can feel my face contort. "Uh, yes. I think I'll be OK."

"These are excellent seats. Half court, eight rows up. I know you've been wanting to go for awhile now, and I wanted to surprise you. You'll be able to see the sweat beads off Hardin's forehead with these seats."

"Thank you. That's very thoughtful." I love all sports, just as much as the next man. And these are some really good seats. I'd love to go under any other circumstances but this one. But I will do my best to enjoy it. Just as long as Terrance doesn't try to touch me, we'll be OK.

When we finally get to our seats, the jump ball has already been won by our home team and they've made a quick two points. The crowd is ramped up as usual in their sea of red and I'm looking forward to a big win. The game is exciting and I'm having a good time watching the lead swing back and forth between the two teams. I can normally hold off till the fourth quarter to use the bathroom, but Nicole's bladder won't allow that. Four minutes before half time, I'm headed to the women's restroom. The line is already long, and I glance at the men's bathroom but know there's no way I could slip in and out without being noticed. I won't even chance that. I'll just have to wait. I look at my phone to avoid eye contact. I really don't feel like talking. I text Nicole to see what she's doing but she doesn't reply right away. An older lady in front of me keeps making comments, trying to get me or anyone close to her to talk. I'm not biting. I look at all the women, some with kids, waiting. Despite the long line it's moving at a steady pace. I finally get around the corner and into the bathroom. I thought there would be a gathering of women chit chatting in the corner or something and some tying up the mirrors, but they are surprisingly very efficient.

I get back to my seat and Terrance hands me some French fries. We're up by 17 points at the start of the third quarter but that doesn't mean much. That lead can be blown at any time when you're up against the Spurs. There's so much energy in the stadium. There seems to be more San Antonio fans than usual tonight, which is abnormal, even though they only have to travel three hours to get here.

Terrance and I are enjoying the game, having a great conversation about the players, stats, and the teams' chances in the playoffs. I notice him staring at me through my peripheral vision. I pretend to be oblivious. Maybe Nicole isn't this knowledgeable or fanatical about basketball. I may need to tone it down a notch.

"I didn't know you were as into sports as I was. I feel like I'm with one of the guys; you really know your stuff," he smiles.

I respond with a half-smile and a head nod and return my focus back to the game.

"Whoa!" I jump up, spilling some of my soda because he rubs his hand on the inside of my thigh. *Hold up partner.*

"What's wrong?"

*Don't punch him. You're Nicole, he thinks you're Nicole,* I say to myself. "I'm going to the concession stand, you want anything?" I don't wait for an answer. It'll take too long for his mouth to close. I know he's confused. He was too comfortable putting his hand on Nicole's leg, so He's used to doing this. That mean's…I don't want to even think about it. Now I'm angry and ready to go. I'll just stay at the top of the stairs and watch the rest of the game.

On the way home. I'm silent. I can tell he's trying to think of something to say and retrace his steps to figure out what he did wrong.

"Uh, what happened back there? Did I say something or—"

"Nah Dog, you're good," I say without thinking. Uh oh, not good.

"Where did that come from? Who have you been hanging around lately?"

"Oh, sorry. I hear these interns talk like that. I guess I picked up some of their slang, just by osmosis."

He shakes his head. "You must have picked up more than their slang. You haven't been yourself for a while."

"I've just been under a lot of pressure, but I'll be fine."

"Well, how bad could it be? I'm under constant pressure at my job. You've just got to learn to leave it at the office and not let it affect you."

I grunt under my breath. You have no idea. I turn to him. How do you handle leaving your penis at the office? He scrunches his face at me. Did I say that out loud? Wait, no I didn't, but he sure is looking at me like he heard me. I burst out laughing.

He's confused but chuckles half-hearted anyway. He must think Nicole has gone crazy. That starts me laughing again. Now he's fidgeting in his seat and I'm trying to keep my composure. Now I know how hard it is not to laugh at the very moment you're not supposed to. I'm remembering the faces of the youth in church when you can tell they're trying to suppress their laughter but can barely keep it held in. I feel just like them. I'm rubbing my forehead, pursing my lips. What is wrong with me?

"We're here."

*Oh, thank you Jesus.* I literally squeak out a 'thank you' and exit the car without giving him a chance to say or do anything more. Three steps toward the front door and I can't hold it in any longer. I let it all out. I laugh like a little school girl, a laugh that comes from the belly. I'm so loud that I stay outside the building to finish. The few people out here may think I'm drunk, but I don't care. I need this laugh.

When I do make it to Nicole's condo, I don't think I'm there five minutes before she calls. I click the green button. "There's a 50/50 chance your man will call you back."

"What? Wait, what do you mean? What happened?"

"You'd better talk to your man, and tell him to keep his hands to himself."

She laughs. "You're me, you've got to do it, Silly."

"OK, keep laughing, when he comes up missing, don't say I didn't warn you. I can't do this again. I'm telling you. I'm sorry, whatever happens, happens. If he dumps you, it just wasn't meant to be. Somebody else will come along, but I can't do this."

"I'd do it for you."

"Yeah, well I did it for you, but that's it."

"Well, why do you sound so happy about it?"

"Sometimes you've got to laugh to keep from crying."

# 31 Darnell

I ARRIVE AT a local coffee shop. I want to sit down and clear my head. I have so much to think about. I'm frustrated that things aren't back to normal. I look up and see a few of my church leaders eating together. One of my trustees, Brother Larkin notices me, well Nicole, and waves me over.

"Sister Nicole, come join us."

"Hi. Brother Larkin, Deacon Joe, Brother Gladwell. What are you up to?"

"As a matter of fact, we're talking about the church."

"Oh, OK. Is something wrong?" I sit in the empty chair.

"How do you think things are going at the church?" Deacon Joe asks.

"Just fine." I say, but something's not right, I can tell.

"It's been almost two years since Pastor Andrews left us, God rest his soul. But the processes he put in place are working just fine. He was from the old school. He knew how to get things done. And I don't see why we need to change anything. If it 'aint broke don't fix it," Bro. Larkin says.

"Pastor Thompson, don't get me wrong, he means well and has a good heart, I can tell that, but what is he, thirty-six, thirty-seven?" Bro Gladwell asks.

"Can't be more than forty," Bro. Larkin says.

"He's thirty-three." I correct.

"OK thirty-three. He's a young buck. I can still smell the milk on his breath. Now, he's taking a risk with the whole church. This is an established congregation. We've all been here for twenty, thirty years and you shouldn't just change what's working," Bro. Larkin says.

"I know he wants to make his mark, but it seems he's hell bent on erasing Pastor Andrews's legacy," Bro. Gladwell adds.

"But we're not perfect. We can stand to make some improvements." I remind them.

"No more annual days, one hundred men in black, he got rid of Texas and Louisiana Day, the Heaven or Hell cook-off...why get rid of stuff we've been doing for years? People look forward to that," Bro. Larkin says.

"We're transitioning from being a church that's just satisfied to come fellowship and do church as usual Sunday after Sunday, to a church that actually does the work of the church; evangelism, ministry, outreach. We're making great progress."

"Sister, that was a thorough answer. And I think we all would agree with you on the ministry aspect, but that doesn't mean you have to get rid of the fun stuff," Bro. Gladwell says.

"I just want to usher the church into the 21st century," I slip. They all look at me. "…that's a direct quote." That seems to appease them. "He doesn't intend to wipe out everything, he just wants to implement some new processes and new leaders. Change things up a bit so we won't get stagnant."

"Why are you so gung ho all of a sudden? You were the main one who was against the light show he wants to install," Bro. Larkin asks.

"No, I was the only one who spoke up. If you felt the same way you should have said something. Why did you leave me hanging out there by myself like I was the only one who had a problem with some of the changes? You guys need to speak up. You make me look like I'm just complaining." Heads nodding and shifting gestures is all I get in response. "Say something."

"It is what it is. You know how pastors are. They're going to do what they want to regardless," Deacon Joe finally comments.

"The pastor needs to know when you don't like something, or else he'll think everything's fine. Don't wait until after the fact to say you didn't agree with something. At least Nic—, at least I have the courage to stand up for what I believe."

172

"No matter what any of us say, all a pastor has to say is they feel God is leading them in such and such direction, and that's that." Bro. Gladwell adds.

"You can't compete with that," Bro. Larkin says.

"Who are we to question that?" Bro. Gladwell throws his hands up.

"Pastors aren't perfect. They do make mistakes," I offer.

"So, what do you want us to do, tell him he didn't hear from God? Come on," Bro. Larkin grunts.

"You might as well call him a liar, cause that's just what you're saying if we say that to him," Deacon Joe says.

I'm taken aback by all of this. Am I that bad that they would rather use Nicole as a sounding board than level with me? I hear what they're saying but they still could have come to me no matter how difficult the conversation would have been. Even if I didn't agree with them, at least they would have my respect. But Nicole did come to me, openly and behind closed doors, but I don't think I gave her much of it. She deserves more. This realization hits me in the pit of my stomach. God is no respecter of persons, and neither should I.

# 32 Darnell

AFTER THE REALIZATION of how unfair I've been to Nicole, my guilt makes me do something I said I wouldn't do again…go out with her boyfriend. I meet Terrance at the restaurant. He begged to come get me but I'm not going to be cooped up in a car with him. The least amount of time I spend with him the better. I'm tired of this. The only reason why I even agreed to this date is because Nicole begged me to at least let him know that she still values their relationship. I'm being pressured by both of them. I've got to compromise somewhere though, since I was adamant about not talking on the phone with him. He's really being patient with her, I've got to give him that. He bought all the excuses about sickness, the big work project, and having to meet deadlines. There's only so much more we can come up with, that's believable anyway. Nicole loves the guy, and I owe her one, that's the only reason I agree to do this.

He told me to meet him at Phil and Derek's. I've never been but I've heard a lot of nice things about the establishment. At least the evening won't be a total waste of my time. I told him I'd only go under one condition; no physical contact. He nearly blew a gasket. I made up something about him touching or kissing me would only make me vulnerable so those are the conditions I need to avoid temptation. Anyway, he bought it; he had no choice.

I see him from the parking lot. He's wearing a cool shirt and slacks. He cleans up well. Nicole wanted me to wear a dress and some heels. Not a chance. I wanted to wear a shirt and jeans, and tennis shoes. I came close. She picked out what she calls a blouse, which she made sure was low cut. She said she wanted to keep him interested and remind him of what he was waiting for. And instead of tennis shoes, I compromised on loafers. She did her own hair and makeup, so her face looks gorgeous. When I looked in the mirror I suggested that she not make herself look too good, but of course she ignored me.

I walk up to him and he just stares at me. *I knew this was too much.* He leans in, but I turn my body and arch my eyebrows. If he doesn't understand my body language, he sure understands my face. *OK man, remember what I said on the phone.* He reaches for my hand and kisses the top of it. I swallow my objection and take one for the team. *You owe me bigtime, Nicole.*

Terrance had already made reservations, so we don't wait long. I can hear the live jazz music around a corner as we're being ushered to our table. He says he has already ordered our appetizers, so the waitress quickly brings a dish of Crawfish Mac & Cheese Balls. They taste pretty good. When the waitress comes back to check if we need drink refills, she mentions that our entrées will be right out, but I hadn't ordered anything. I look at Terrance for an explanation.

"Oh, I took the liberty and ordered for you. I know what you like."

"Oh, really? OK" I'm a little disappointed I won't be able to choose from the menu, but I'll go with it.

"Yeah, you normally get the Blackened Shrimp and Grits."

"So, what did you get?"

"Filet Mignon with mashed potatoes and green beans."

Well, why not? "That's fine." I say.

Over dinner he talks about work and asks about my project, which I overly hype up as being strenuous and requiring a lot of long hours. I notice him fidget with his collar a bit. He must feel threatened by Nicole's job. I need to change the subject; I don't feel like being quizzed tonight. With his lawyer background, I can't afford to trip up and say something wrong. I'm sure Nicole didn't tell me the smallest details that I need to know. And even if she did, I don't know if I even remember them. I see different games on the TV screens from afar, so I try to make safe conversation about that.

Everything is going well. The food arrives quickly, so I expect to be out of here soon.

"Let's pray," he says.

176

This takes me by surprise because he doesn't seem like the type of person to pray in public. He reaches for my hand, which is safely under the table. *OK I'm used to holding hands and praying with people. I can do this.* I pull my hand out and place it in his. His prayer is short and to the point, which I am grateful for, so we eat.

The food is amazing, I must say. I'll definitely be coming back to this spot. After the waitress removes our dinner plates, she smiles at Terrance and glances at me. That's pretty bold on her part but she can flirt with him all she wants, I don't care. I make chit chat about how wonderful of an evening it has been, but my voice is being drowned out by the sounds of a saxophone playing Stevie Wonder's, Ribbon in the Sky. I turn and see the player moving past each table, a nice touch for the couples. Nicole would have enjoyed this.

As the saxophonist gets to our table, I nod my head in recognition of his talent, but I don't think that gives him an invitation to linger in front of us.

"Nicole? Nicole?"

I turn to Terrance and my face must have turned pale. I gasp and sink into the chair. *Oh, my God. No, no, no.* Terrance is staring at me, but he's holding a small black box. No, this can't be happening. What am I going to do? This man is about to propose. My mind blocks out whatever he's saying. I can't say yes. Nicole would want me to, but I can't. I can't let her miss this moment. Women remember this moment for the rest of their lives, I can't do that to her.

I can't say no either. I keep my head straight but look around the room, I feel like everything is in slow motion. I see different women at their tables gawking over what they deem a romantic gesture. I see men nodding their heads in approval or simply smiling. Everyone is waiting for my answer. If I say no, his pride will take a beating, one that I don't know if he'll ever recover from. If I say yes, I guess Nicole can tell him no later, so he won't be embarrassed…wait, but she won't say no later. I'm sure she's been wanting this, probably praying for it, so who am I to stand in the way of her happiness? Oh, no. If I say yes, he'll expect a kiss, and not on the forehead or cheek either. Well, that settles it.

"I'm so sorry. I know that I love you, but I just can't give you an answer right now," I reply.

"Why not?"

*Because you're just not the right man for her. I don't even know what Nicole see's in you,* I wish I could tell him. "I'm just not myself. I'm going through so many emotions, and this is just too much for me right now."

"All you have to do is say yes. You love me, and I love you so what else is there to consider?"

"I don't know. My mind is confused. I just need time to sort things out." I feel extremely hot and look for something to fan myself. I notice all these people quickly look away from me as I squirm.

"Why are you avoiding looking at me? It's your pastor isn't it?"

"What?" I'm dumbfounded that I would even be mentioned in this conversation. "What does this have to do with him?"

"You've been spending too much time with him. Every time I look up, you're with him."

OK, this conversation is taking a turn. He closes the box and puts it in his pocket. "I'm the secretary, so I do a lot for the church. I'm basically like his personal assistant."

"I'm no fool. A normal secretary doesn't spend that much time with the pastor, no matter how much you're doing."

I choose to ignore his statement. "Our church is going through a lot of transition. He's making some changes and it's requiring me to spend more time than usual. But I promise things will get back to normal."

"When?"

"Soon, I hope."

"Doesn't he know you have a man and a life?" he asks rhetorically. "You're not even getting paid for what you do there. That church is taking advantage of you." He pauses just long enough to throw another zinger at me. "And you have no feelings for him whatsoever?"

He said it as a statement instead of a question. I raise an eyebrow. Does Nicole have feelings for me? Nah, she's never done or said anything to make me think otherwise. "No, not that I'm aware of."

"What is that supposed to mean?"

"I mean, I've never looked at him in that way."

"Well, does he have feelings for you? Is that why he wants you around him all the time?"

"I don't know." *Do I have feelings for Nicole? She is a beautiful woman but*—Terrance's strong gaze abruptly pulls me back. I need to give a better answer than that. "He's never given me any indication that he has any feelings for me whatsoever, so I don't think so."

His ego is still bruised so I say, "I really thank you for all the effort you put into making this evening so special. And I'm sorry I didn't give you an answer, but I know you want me to be honest with my feelings no matter how much it may hurt, right?"

"OK. You need more time, I'll give you more time." He leans in to kiss me! I almost stiff arm him.

"Nicole, what is with you?"

"I need to keep my mind clear, that's all."

"Nicole, I'm a man, I have needs. We haven't slept together in a while. One day you say you're sick, then you say you've made a vow to be celibate, which I thought was a ploy to get me to propose. Now, I've proposed, and you still don't want to be intimate. That's not normal. What is it you're not telling me?"

"I'm a woman and I have needs too, one of which is for you not to pressure me into doing something that I don't want to do."

"Oh, you want to. You be wanting it just as much as I do, but now all of a sudden you just shut it off, out of nowhere. You've changed just that fast. It'd be different if that's been our relationship all along, but we've been doing it on a regular, and now, nothing. How is that fair to me?"

"I've grown, and I just want to do it right. I have that choice."

"That church or that pastor has gotten into your head, and you fell for it."

"Where is this coming from? You go to church and read the bible just like I do. It's in there."

"Did that new pastor make it a rule or something that people in a position have to be held to some sort of double standard than the rest of the members?"

"What?"

"Like you can't have sex unless you're married…nobody's perfect Nicole. And if your pastor thinks the single people at his church aren't having sex…he's crazy."

Not a bad idea. People in leadership should be held to a higher standard.

"Nicole!"

"Huh? No, no, the pastor's never said anything like that. But what if he did? I mean doesn't your church teach about fornication?"

"God already knows what we're going to do before we do it. I'm not the first one to do it, and I won't be the last. David slept with a woman and killed her husband, but he's called A Man After God's Own Heart so, come on, what's worse?"

I refrain from shaking my head. He's not the only one who thinks like that; there's so many people who have the same mindset, justifying their sin. They look at David's indiscretion but ignore his repentance and thirst for God. They forget David still had to face the consequences of his actions; not only did his baby die, but the sword never left his household. You may be able to pick the sin, but you can't pick the consequences. My explanation will fall on deaf ears. I'm ready to go though. *Sorry, Nicole but I'm about to make him mad.* "So that's the reason you proposed. Because you think, now we can have all the sex you want?" I don't even wait for a response. I snatch the napkin off my lap, toss it on the table and charge toward the door. "Good night Mr. Miller."

"Nicole."

He only calls her name once, but I never look back. When I drive away I still see no sign of him. Good. The less that happens, the less I have to remember to tell Nicole. She's not going to like it, but I did what I had to. But I won't be calling her tonight, I've had enough for one day.

# 33 Darnell

THE BIG PRESENTATION is this afternoon. With not much time for a lunch break, Nicole meets me at a small sandwich shop a block from her building. It's crowded and joined to other eating establishments in a set-up that resembles a food court in a mall or airport. Everyone is occupied doing something; talking to a colleague, looking at their laptops or a set of binders or papers they've pulled from their briefcases, all while getting bites of food or spoons of soup in between. Most of the patrons seem busy and feel a bit rushed, including us.

Nicole and I push our plates of the little that's left of our sandwich and fries. Nicole is walking me through the finishing touches on a proposal she's put together for her boss and the important client. She's grilling me, asking me questions she anticipates her boss and others will throw at me this afternoon. I feel confident in what we've gone over the last few days and even these last-minute additions are manageable with my notes.

I see him first since Nicole's back is to the front door; Terrance coming our way with a look on his face that says, "well ain't this a beast."

I instantly regret not telling Nicole about the engagement. I was going to tell her after I finished the presentation to the client. I didn't want her to lose focus on her thoughts while preparing it nor me for the big task. And I didn't think Terrance would try and reach her, let alone in person, until at least later tonight or tomorrow. Since he didn't call her phone last night, I figured he would wait a day or so before trying to reach her. By then, she would have been past the need to be able to concentrate on this without interruption or the feelings that come with the fact that your boyfriend proposed but your pastor said no on your behalf.

I only have about ten seconds to tell her something so she's not completely caught off guard. "Nicole, I'm sorry. Terrance proposed last night. I said no. I was going to tell you later tonight, after all this presentation stuff was finalized. And he's right behind you," I regurgitate.

The news shocks her into silence and freezes her face. Although her eyes and mouth are twice their size, I see her mind calculating, probably pondering whether to punch me or turn and run into Terrance's arms. Of course, she can do neither, so she closes her eyes and braces herself for the impact.

He nonchalantly walks up to our table. "You don't have time to eat lunch with me, but you find time to eat with your boyfriend huh?" His voice is calm. When I instinctively glance at Nicole, Terrance quips, "What are you looking at him for?"

"Hi Terrance," Nicole turns to him and she can't hide the longing in her voice…my voice. If he were to look back at her, and really look into her eyes, he'd be able to see her, feel her, even though she's in my body. But he's too angry for that to happen.

"Terrance, this is not my boyfriend. This is a business meeting, nothing more," I say. This seems to snatch Nicole out of her stupor.

Terrance quickly tries to lift the presentation I had placed face down on the table. Nicole quickly pushes her hand on the top, slamming it back down. "Sorry brother, this is confidential church business. No disrespect." If he were to see the charts and graphs, it would be hard to explain why Nicole was talking to her pastor about a job presentation.

Terrance narrows his eyes at who he thinks is me. "Did she tell you I asked her to marry me?"

I know this is a test to see how much Nicole shares with me. "No, she didn't. Congratulations," Nicole wisely replies.

"No Reverend, she said 'No.'"

I look at my body as Nicole raises my eyebrows to enhance "my" performance. "Oh, really?" she says in my voice. "Well maybe just give her some time. I'm sure she'll come around, must have a lot on her mind." She turns to me and adds, "Maybe you should take a break from the things you do for me at the church, so you can have time to think." She then returns to Terrance and assures him, "I'm sure the next time you ask her, you'll get a different answer."

Terrance looks at Nicole's body, which I am trying my best to look dignified but also apologetic. "I hope so, because I won't ask again," he scoffs. As he walks off, out of the corner of my eye I see my mouth open and then I stare into my own eyes. *So, this is what I look like when I'm sad.*

Nicole shakes her head, asking without words, *how could you?* But instead of addressing it she looks at the watch on her wrist and says, "we'll talk about this later. I want to know everything that happened, and I mean everything." She turns the notes back over and goes through them with me. I'm soaking up every word she utters, while finalizing this presentation prep, but I can still see a tear fall as she quickly wipes it away.

# 34 Darnell

I STEP INTO the conference room after praying again at Nicole's desk. I've delivered many sermons to different sizes of congregations and I make sure to prepare my best with all of them, no matter the size. I prepare and pray. Sometimes I preach with more notes than at other times, but I always rely on the Holy Spirit to give me the words and to fill me with his anointing as I stand up before the people. Being in sales before, I know there's a difference, but it still takes both, preparation and prayer. I walk over to Nicole's laptop and double check everything; my slides are displayed on the wall-mounted screen and my paper presentations are in a pile ready for me to distribute to all the attendees plus a couple extra. There will be three in all: Nicole's boss, Gary, Dillon, the owner of the software company, our potential client, and Susan, their HR Director, whom if they sign with us, I, well Nicole, would be working closely with going forward. I look over the notes, including the additional ones Nicole gave me at lunch. I look at the clock on the far wall and compare it to Nicole's watch to make sure it's accurate. If it were my own eyes, I wouldn't be able to see the etches on this tiny watch. I remember the time is also on the bottom of the screen on the laptop, but I'm not used to that. I don't have that on Sunday mornings, so I know I'll forget and resort to my habit of looking at the biggest timepiece in the room. It's a little after 2pm and I can hear Gary and the client making their way to the room.

We exchange pleasantries and Dillon reiterates to Gary a broad picture of what his company is looking for and where he sees his firm in the years to come. Susan interjects some points and I'm nodding my head and taking notes. Nicole's boss restates how we continue to work with heavy hitters in the industry and the value our Staffing Agency can bring to their organization. It's a nice segue to my presentation and I take it from there. I lean into my prior sales experience and my practice with Nicole and roll through several slides until I'm interrupted yet again, but this time with a question by their director, that I don't have a clue how to answer. I don't even understand the question, so I ask Susan to repeat it. When she does, I look at Gary for assistance. He adjusts himself in his chair, explains her question, waits for the answer from me, which never comes, then he answers it himself with a percentage range. That one moment is the turning point of the entire meeting. They have uncovered my weakness, which makes them second guess me as a representative of the company and causes them to go over the rest of the entire presentation with a fine-tooth comb.

Thirty minutes into the presentation, the owner gives Susan a knowing look, which Gary picks up on. He sits back in his chair and says we should take a short break. He now gets up and asks to have a word with me outside the room. He takes quick strides to his office which is a couple doors from the conference room and closes the door.

"Nicole, what is wrong with you? You've completely lost them. They've lost confidence in you and frankly, so have I. You don't know your numbers. You don't have the answers to most of their questions and you seem discombobulated."

"Yeah, I know. I got thrown off."

"Nicole, this is the big time. They are a huge potential client, you know that. We don't have any room for error."

I shake my head. He folds his arms and looks down at the floor while he taps his fingers on his arm.

"Nicole, I'm taking over the meeting. At this point, I think that's the best course of action. You can go to your office and wait for me there. I don't think you should come back in."

I'm stunned, but what else can I do? I simply say, "I respect your decision, Gary."

***

I pace the floor in Nicole's office for a while in case Gary changes his mind and lets me go back into the meeting. Although, I don't know if I want to go back. I don't want to screw it up any more than I already have. I feel bad for the client, Gary, and most importantly Nicole. I've let everyone down. Fifteen minutes have passed. It's safe to say, he won't be coming back to include me, so I go take a walk to clear my head. I peer over the rows of cubicles in the middle of the office to see if anyone is eyeing me, realizing what just happened to my big opportunity. No one is standing or lollygagging. I don't know if I'm being paranoid, but I don't even hear the typical office chatter that accompanies the afternoon air. I go to the break room and get some water. This is where I see everyone, eating cake. It's someone's birthday. I turn to leave but get called out.

"Nicole, I thought you were in the meeting with the big software company."

"I am." I quickly turn without giving an explanation. I leave them with the puzzled look on their face.

It's safer back in Nicole's office. I wait for almost an hour for Gary and the client to leave the conference room. I debate over and over whether to call Nicole, but I don't need her screaming in my ear and worried about her job. If she gets let go, worrying isn't going to help her get it back. I don't think she's crazy enough to come up here in my body and as a pastor beg for a "parishioner" to keep her job, but I don't put it past her. She kept reminding me how big of an opportunity it is to present to this prestigious client and how much new business this could bring to her firm and of course a big raise and a promotion for her. I tried my best to do everything she told me. I know how much this means to her. But none of that matters; I blew it anyway. Lord, why did you allow me to mess up like that? I don't know what happened. I studied the material, I thought I knew it inside and out, but they didn't ask the questions quite like Nicole did when we practiced. They fired them off like machine-gun pellets, one right after another. I barely had time to answer one person's question before another came rushing in. And they asked the most obscure questions: what does that number mean on graph 5 of page 1 compared to this number on chart 4 of page 8, explain the temp vs permanent percentages and their contributions to the company's forecasted revenues and how I thought the increase in the unemployment rate would affect contract margins and perm fees, and how would I do this and that. I looked at the presentation and my notes and the words on the page got blurry. I looked at Nicole's boss for help and he did pitch in a few answers, but I had to tell them more times than I can count that I'd have to get back to them with the answer. I was completely out of my element. I'd rather study Greek and Hebrew Bible manuscripts. And then I just got nervous and one mistake led to another. That was a disaster. I hold my head in my hands and massage my temples.

I hear a knock on the door and I brace myself as Gary enters. "This is the worst presentation you've ever given. You didn't know the material. You didn't remember simple facts about the company and you've worked here for years. Nicole, this is not you at all. What is going on?"

I search my mind for any explanation. I didn't' think of one in the hour that I was sitting here so I don't know why I expect to find one now. I jump out of my seat. "I don't know. I'm very sorry. What did they say?"

He rolls his eyes. "I have to do some damage control." He paces the floor.

I don't know whether I should be talking or not. It may make things worse; if that's even possible. But with all that Nicole has done for this company, surely—

"Nicole, I'm going to have to ask you to leave."

"You're firing me?"

"Someone in HR will be in touch with you."

Before I can say anything more, he turns and leaves.

Oh my God, what have I done? My knees weaken. I fall into the chair stunned and defeated.

# 35 Nicole

I AM LIVID. Darnell got me fired! I can't believe it. I'm speechless. There's got to be something he's not telling me. Could he have been that bad that Gary stopped him in the middle of his presentation? I've never seen that happen before. I don't even have words. He must have made me look like a total imbecile. I don't know who to be mad at most, Darnell for getting me fired, or Gary for firing me after one mess-up. I am an exemplary employee. I've worked hard for this company, gone above and beyond, treated it like it was my own. How can they treat me like this? Darnell may have blown it with one of our biggest potential clients but come on. They're throwing me away like a paper towel. I've been more than loyal to them; staying late, working on the weekends. And now I'm dispensable.

This is the last thing I expected to happen. I'm supposed to be toasting in celebration of landing one of my biggest clients. Instead, my mind is racing about what to do next. I feel like I've been tossed by a tornado I never saw coming.

I can't even talk to anyone about this because I'm not even me. I feel pain on the side of my forehead. I have a piercing headache. *Lord, I need your help. Why did you let this happen?* I'm too upset to try and find any medicine. I let my head fall into my hands and try to forget it all.

***

I'm frustrated with God. Notwithstanding my now uncertain career, I don't know why he hasn't answered my prayer yet. Well he may have, but it certainly hasn't been manifested into me getting back in my own body. I leave Pastor's house, my temporary abode that seems less temporary with every passing day, and just drive around the city. I feel lost, not physically lost, I mean I know where I am and how to get back to his house, I feel spiritually lost, drained even. Cars are honking as they speed around me. I sigh. I know I need to get off the road because of the emotional state I'm in. If I were following a driver like me, I'd be upset too. I drive a while longer until I see a spot where I can pull over…a small park. There are only a few cars in the parking lot. The sun is still on duty, so I reach for pastor's cap and sunglasses and get out to walk the trails and release some of my frustration. I'm tired of being this way. *Why Lord, why? What am I supposed to get out of this? What kind of test is this? I want to pass, so please tell me what I'm supposed to learn.* I keep walking, which turns into a jog, and eventually I run. I rush past other people sprinkled along the trail, past the benches and the occasional green trash can. As I run, my anger is sparked, so I keep running. Even though I can see the cars piled into three steady lines of red lights along the street that borders the outer edge of the park, I can no longer hear their noise. I can't even hear the sound of the kid bouncing a ball on the pavement, nor his mother's words as she tries to get his attention. I can only see her mouth move. I've done a few laps by now, which I mark each time I pass by the pastor's car and notice the parking lot is now three-fourths full. I glance at Pastor's watch, which would be too big to fit on my own arm. I've been out here for at least forty-five minutes. I make a note to make sure I stop at the water fountain when I get to it again.

I don't know what else to do, don't know what else to pray, so I switch my attention to what I need to make sure is done at the job and anything I need to tell the pastor about the church. I'm thirstier than I thought but I can see the fountain in the distance, so I start to slow my pace. *Wait, what the*—I blink rapidly. I don't believe my eyes. My body comes to a halt. I wipe the sweat from my eyes and hope I'm hallucinating.

Not even twenty feet away, is a woman sitting on a bench, her legs crossed and body leaning into the chest of my man! I only see the side of his face, but I know it's him. His arm is propped around her shoulder. I stand there. My eyes widen, and my heart is beating faster with each second that passes. All the anger that I just ran out, that I grinded out of me with every foot I pounded on this ground, comes crashing back to me. He doesn't even look up.

"Excuse me, Sir," an elderly person bumps into me, which reminds me of who's body I'm in.

The sound of my heart is pounding between my ears, in lock step with my stride. I get right up on them. "What are you doing?"

Terrance looks at the woman. "Do you know this cat?"

"No," she says, scrunching her eyebrows.

With that, Terrance leans away from her. "What's up Man?"

"So, this is how you treat Nicole!" I don't wait for his eyes to get any bigger. I've already cocked my arm back and planted my knuckles into his face. Her scream just makes me angrier and I hit him two or three more times before someone pushes me off him. "You low life. After, everything she's done for you? You don't deserve her!" I come to myself as I realize two men are steadily pushing me away from him. "Alright, alright. I'm sorry, I'm sorry." I say in a hushed tone. I'm winded but I keep my eyes on Terrance and that woman, who is no doubt asking him what's going on. I raise my hands to my capturers, letting them know I'm serious about my surrender. I want to tell them thank you for pulling me off him but if I speak, I will burst into tears. I am overwhelmed with emotion and fight the urge to hug one of them. I need to get out of here. I look to the sky so I won't cry, and walk to my car. I can hardly see through the puddles that have collected in my eyes. As if on cue, as soon as I slam the car door, the dam breaks. I scream, and the tears won't stop.

# 36 Darnell

I FINISH LIFTING weights in the condominium's work out room. Even though it's not helping my own physical body, I need to keep some type of workout routine and it helps me think. I'm sure Nicole won't object when she she's the outcome. I remember to wear her sports bra but maneuvering around her chest while lifting the weights takes some time getting used to, especially using the lat machine and tricep rope.

I've got to hand it to Nicole. She has very nice taste. I'm sure she did a lot of research before picking this property to stay in. They have several helpful amenities, but I'm sure she pays a pretty penny for all the perks. I stop at the restaurant downstairs and pick up my to-go order. I return to Nicole's condo within minutes. I situate myself at the table and turn on the TV. I'm eating a bowl of soup as I attempt to watch the news, so I can stay informed on current events and catch up on the sports scene. What I see causes me to drop my spoon. I shake my head and shoot up from the chair. *Wait, Lord this can't be real.* I see myself assaulting another man. "Wait, that's Terrance!"

I grab the phone to get some answers.

"Nicole, what is going on? Why did you punch Terrance?"

"I was going to tell you. I mean, it just happened. Wait, how do you know about it? He called you?"

"It's on the news!"

"Impossible. I mean…uh…how?"

"Well, someone videotaped it and sent it to the news station. Nicole, what happened?"

"He cheated on me."

"I'm sorry Nicole."

"I caught him with a woman right there in the park."

"Nicole, I truly am sorry but why did you have to involve me in it?"

"I wasn't thinking about that. I wasn't thinking at all. All I saw was him with another woman."

"So, what do you want me to do when he calls?"

"And why would he call?"

"Nicole, trust me, he's going to call."

"Block his number."

"OK."

"Wait. Then he won't be able to leave a message."

"What?"

"Don't answer, just keep sending him to voicemail. Let him leave a message. I just want to know why."

"Right. Nicole, I know you're hurting, if there's anything else I can do, let me know. I'm not trying to make this about me, but I've got to bring it up…what if Terrance decides to sue me over this?"

"He won't. His pride won't let him."

"Don't be too sure about that. Nicole, this is going to be a problem. If I saw it, other people are going to see it as well, and this doesn't look good at all. I'll…I'll talk to you tomorrow." I'm too upset to talk further so I hang up and ponder what to do next.

# 37 Nicole

I'M STARING AT the wall. Darnell was right. I have created a huge problem. A member of our church board called because they have been made aware of the airing of the incident and the situation 'needs to be dealt with' in his words. I am so embarrassed, and I don't know what to do. I've sat here long enough for an idea, any idea, to come to me, but none has. This issue isn't going away so I call Darnell.

"Yes?"

His greeting isn't rude, but it isn't inviting either, so I get right to it. "Darnell, I just got a call. The elders of the church board want to meet with me, well with you, the pastor, over the video."

"I figured that was coming."

"I didn't want to ask the minister who called me any questions that you should already know the answers to."

"Who called?"

I look at the name and number I had scribbled down. "Minister Thaddeus."

"Minister Thaddeus. I haven't had many interactions with him, but I know who he is."

"So, what does this all mean?"

"Many churches have boards that are formed to handle church-minister relations, like searching for a new minister, or establishing the pastor's salary, if he gets one; most pastors in small churches don't. They also deal with negative things like deciding what to do with a pastor who has had an indiscretion of some kind."

"What's going to happen?"

"They want to hear my side of the story."

"Who all is going to be there?"

"Normally a board is made up of leaders, whether it be elders, deacons, or other ministers, that are members of that specific church, but Pastor Andrews had it set up in the church by-laws to have the board consist of pastors that served with him in the fellowship of churches our church is part of."

"Why would he have people from the outside determine what happens in our church?"

"It's actually a wise move. It protects the church from having a pastor that is unfit and prevents the possibility of him manipulating the process by appointing people who would favor him or be selfishly motivated to support him to the detriment of the church. Also, it's to avoid impartiality from any power group that may form within the church, who may have ulterior motives for trying to get rid of the pastor. And only another pastor can truly understand the weight of their decision and its impact on a fellow laborer."

"And what if they don't like what they hear?"

"They'll determine whether or not to discipline me for the misconduct. They can suspend me or fire me."

"They'd fire you over this?"

"Pastors have been fired for a lot less, believe me."

"I'm so sorry. I don't know what else to say or how to fix this."

Darnell doesn't respond. "Please say something," I ask.

"When is the meeting?"

"Wednesday, at the church, but way before Bible Study."

"That's all you have to say?"

"OK...You should feel sorry. I'm the one who has to wade through this mess. This is the type of thing that follows you around forever, long after we get back into our own bodies. It's one thing to hear a rumor and wonder if it's true or not, but to see something with your own eyes on the news is a totally different ballgame. And people can be unforgiving when it comes to the clergy."

"Yeah, I get it. I understand."

"Well, it's best we get prepared for it."

"Whatever you need me to do, I'll do."

"I wish you would have thought about that sooner. You were so hell bent on wanting to inflict pain on Terrance, you didn't even think of what it would do to me. You can't just do anything you want to. Everyone's watching."

"How was I supposed to know someone would be recording it or even know who you are? And then be dirty enough to turn it in to a news station?"

"You don't. That's why you always have to assume someone is. That's the way this works. The world is itching for a negative story, especially one on a pastor, and you just gave them exactly what they want. Nicole, you've damaged me and the church's reputation."

I feel like less than dirt. I never meant for any of this to happen and I definitely didn't want to drag Darnell's name into this mess. But I truly believe if he were to catch someone he loved cheating, he'd do something he would regret as well, whether finding out behind closed doors or in broad daylight amongst other people. You don't know how you'll react when someone rips your heart out of your chest. A few punches in the face is nothing compared to what Terrance did to me. And his wounds will heal much faster than mine.

# 38 Nicole

PASTOR AND I sit in the conference room of the church, waiting for the meeting to begin. He's already advised me on what to say and what not to. I look at the wall clock, it's already fifteen minutes past the meeting's start time. The room where we've had so many discussions about church growth campaigns, strategies about various auxiliaries, fundraisers and even funeral arrangements, is now a room where I feel we are standing on trial, and I am the defendant.

The door opens, and a number of people file in, some of which I've never seen. As we had practiced, Darnell greets the ones he knows I've never met by name, and I mimic him. Then he asks them if they'd like some water to drink. They cordially decline.

"Actually, Sister Nicole, we'd like this meeting to just involve the Pastor. Could you wait outside?" Minister Thaddeus asks.

"No, I need her to stay." I say.

"And why is that?"

"To take notes."

"I can assure you, we've got that taken care of."

"And as a witness to what will be discussed in this meeting," I insist, "unless you'd rather me record this proceeding," I add.

"Very well, Pastor Darnell. Let us begin." Thaddeus pauses and continues. "We are disappointed. The incident was caught on video and was aired on the Monday night news. The result of which has cast a negative light on the church."

"Yes, very poor judgement on my part."

"Pastor, it's understandable, not excusable, but not far-fetched to believe that even a pastor could lose his cool in the heat of passion, when you're defending the honor of someone you care about."

Darnell looks at me, dumbfounded. I had called Minister Thaddeus back myself and told him the reason why "I" hit Terrance was because I had caught him cheating on Nicole, and she deserved better than that. I didn't know if the explanation would help but it was the least I could do to try and salvage Darnell's reputation, and his job.

"Thank you for your understanding. It won't happen again."

"But that's not the disturbing part." Thaddeus adjusts his posture. "I got a call from a minister I know who saw the news story, and he claims you used to be his pastor at a church in Georgia. He was trying to reconnect with you, said he'd lost touch after you lost the church."

"I have no idea what you're talking about." I look at Darnell, who shoots out of the chair.

"Pastor Darnell," My head swivels back to the people but I want to scream *Stop*. I want to look back at Darnell and ask him what in the world is going on here. "Let me remind you that when the church search committee started looking for a new pastor after Reverend Andrews passed away, we specifically stated that one of the qualifications of the new pastor was that it must be his first pastorate. That was always Reverend Andrews's request. He had his reasons for this, some may not agree, but he wanted a fresh perspective, and someone his church members could learn from who was not tainted by the traditions and culture of any other congregation. He wanted a candidate with a clean slate."

"Did you, or did you not understand that, and in fact certify you met that and all the other qualifications by signing your name?" Pastor John asks, the first time anyone else besides Minister Thaddeus breaks their silence.

I'm looking like a deer in headlights. I have no idea what's going on or what in the world either one of them is talking about.

"Yes, I did, I mean he did." I hear my real voice say. I turn to look, my mouth open.

"Nicole, why are you speaking for the Pastor?" Thaddeus questions.

"I didn't, I mean Pastor didn't want to say anything, probably because he was afraid."

Heads bobble back and forth to my body then back to who they think is Pastor.

"This is a first, a pastor that doesn't have anything to say, just speechless," Pastor John leans back.

I look at Darnell, my eyes asking; pleading for the truth, any help to set things straight and repudiate their accusations. He closes his eyes, then speaks. "Yes, it's true."

"You seem to be more interested in keeping the pastor's job than he is," Thaddeus's eyebrows scrunch together.

"Well...Pastor poured it out to me one day and He didn't know how to tell the board...The first church he pastored was very short lived, under three months. He was falsely accused of an indiscretion but there was no proof to clear his name so rather than take the time to investigate, the church took the easy way out and washed their hands of the whole situation by letting the pastor go and cutting their losses."

Pastor looks back to me to figure something out to say from the information he's spilling out. Since I'm in his body I need to say something that will make him look like he wants his job. I still have shock plastered on my face, but I manage to regurgitate what was just fed to me and everyone else in the room, by mostly apologizing.

Thaddeus, being the leader of the meeting, looks at his constituents and leans back in his chair. "Pastor Darnell this committee will reconvene in twenty-four hours, which will give us time to individually think about what you've told us. When we come back together we will vote on whether you will remain the pastor of Abiding Grace Church or if you will be relieved of your duties. I thank everyone for their time."

The weight of what he says feels like a ton of bricks bearing down, slowly smothering the breath out of me. There is no talk of discipline, leave of absence, or even an inkling of understanding, just two sides of a coin, keep his job or get fired, that's it, my goodness. As everyone files out, I look at Darnell and see his hope march right out along with the others.

# 39 Nicole

I LOOK INTO his eyes, searching for an explanation.

"Pastor Darnell, what in the world was that all about?"

"I know I messed up."

"But why? Why didn't you just—"

"I've never failed at anything. I fell into a depression and I wanted to distance myself from anyone who knew anything about my past."

"That's why you moved to Texas."

"Yes, I saw an opportunity to start over. God blessed me with this church—"

"No, a lie got you this church. So, it's all about winning with you too? By any means necessary? Lie, cheat, whatever it takes, right? You're just like Terrance."

"It's not what it seems. I didn't set out to deceive anyone."

"How is that? You're telling me you didn't know the qualifications when you applied?"

"Yes, sort of. I was first told about the position when I was finishing up with my biblical studies. One of the professors recommended me to the church when they got wind of them looking. The position wasn't even posted yet. My professor said it would be a great chance for a first-time pastor, but I never knew that it was an actual qualification until I read over the contract, by then it was too late to turn back. I guess everyone assumed I had never been a pastor before because I was just about to graduate. And I figured it wouldn't matter after they saw my heart and passion for them, but I guess not."

"How were you able to pastor without having a divinity degree? Did you lie about that too?"

"No, Nicole. You can be a pastor without having a divinity degree. Look, I know you're still upset about what Terrance did to you but don't project that on to me. He and I are completely different. I know this looks bad, but it's totally different from what he did. I would never cheat on you…I mean…I would never cheat on anyone, no matter who I'm with. It's just not in my character."

"I'm sorry. So, what happened with the first church?"

"I was young and naive. A woman there took interest in me. When I ignored her advances, she had the nerve to accuse me of coming on to her. The pastor, coming on to one of his congregants? Not a good thing."

"Why didn't they believe you?"

"She was an older woman, been at the church for over twenty years. I was a new face. Who were they going to believe? Plus, you'd be surprised at how many people are looking for a good church scandal, especially if it involves the pastor."

"What, you were on the news there too?"

"No, that's the only good part. The church decided to put me away privately."

"Then what do you mean by looking for a church scandal?"

"I'm not talking about society, I'm talking about church folk. They want to see a man fall just like the world. I was naive to think all people who go to church were Christians, but that's not always the case. That was my shock treatment."

"Sounds like a modern-day Mary and Joseph."

"More like Joseph and Potiphar's wife. I was wrongly accused. I did nothing wrong. Now how was I going to even explain this to the committee when they were considering me for this pastorate if I would have been completely transparent and told them about the first church and then they would have asked me why I left? Just think about a secular job, would you hire someone who told you they were wrongfully accused of sexual harassment? Or would you rather go with the candidate who has no baggage, rather than take a chance that might come back to haunt you?"

"Just tell them the truth."

"Nicole, you can be so…Listen, it's good that you still have a sweet, want-to-think-the-best-about-everybody attitude but churches are filled with all kinds of people, some who'd rather believe a lie than the truth any day. And believe it or not, there are far too many people who want to see mess in the church."

"I don't believe that."

"Say what you want, I don't have to believe it, I know it for a fact...I've lived it."

"I'm sorry you had to go through that."

I watch my body take a deep breath. There is nothing left to say. We sit in silence for a long time.

# 40 Nicole

I START TO look up sales positions on a popular recruiting website. It's pretty apropos since this is what my company helps applicants do on a daily basis. Now I'm on the other side of the equation, helping myself. The title I enter returns over five hundred thousand results in Houston. I don't have the energy to do this right now. I fall back in my chair and allow my eyes to wonder around Darnell's room. Even though he lost *my* job, I've got to do everything I can to get his back since my actions were the catalyst for what he's facing now. I just don't know how. My eyes rest on the file cabinet and I open it without even knowing why. I don't normally go through other people's things but maybe something in here will help. I look at the names of each folder and stop at the one titled *Personal*. I lay it on the desk and study its contents. There are certificates of appreciation from his previous sales job, awards, emails, and thank-you letters addressed to him from members at his old church and some from ours. In the back of the folder is a legal sized set of stapled papers that are folded at the bottom to fit the folder. I open the fold. There's a church letterhead that includes a logo, church name, and address. The paper is embossed with the logo as a beautiful watermark. I make a mental note to get something like this for our church. I flip to the back page and see signatures. I go back to the front page and read the whole document. "That's it!" I say aloud. I look at the time on the phone. I run to the kitchen counter and pick up the card Minister Thaddeus, the church moderator, gave me yesterday. I call his cell number, but it goes to voicemail. I call the office number listed and to my disappointment a secretary answers. She says he's in a meeting and I tell her I am on my way. She informs me that he's booked for the day and doesn't see anyone without an appointment. I plead with her to just tell him Pastor Darnell is on the way to show him important paperwork before he makes his final decision. I verify the address, grab the entire folder, and sweep the keys off the counter.

I'm unfamiliar with how to get to Minister Thaddeus's office, especially in this traffic so I must rely on the GPS system. It tells me I won't make it there in time, as the red indicator shows I'll arrive ten minutes later than the 24-hour cut-off time. I speed, but I've never sped for a more noble cause. I start out in line with many cars on the freeway, as I join in the cadence with other offenders who may have their own valid excuses for breaking the law. I glance at the time on the dashboard and my heart beats faster. I smash the gas pedal harder. I'm going so fast, I scare myself, all while constantly praying and looking all around me for any glimpse of a patrol car. The voice on the navigation system directs me to my exit and I comply. I'm now on side streets and the 35 mile an hour speed limit can not be tolerated right now. I'm pushing it to the point that I run orange lights, not yellow. The cameras in the intersection are the only reason I stop at the last light. I find the office building. I jolt the car in park, the back tire straddled over the yellow line, and race to the front steps. I make it to his office with five minutes to spare and slam the folder on the secretary's desk while I catch my breath. I explain who I am, and she sighs and responds, "I'm sorry he's already gone for the day."

"No, no, no!" I slump in the chair in front of her desk. I can no longer hold my body up. I've come too close for things to end this way. I look to her for help but all she does is apologize.

"I did tell him you were on your way."

"How long has he been gone?"

She looks at the clock. "A good 15 minutes."

"Try calling him, please."

She dials the number but his line just rings.

"What kind of car does he drive and where did he park?"

"A dark blue Toyota Camry. He parks in the parking garage in the back of the building." She yells as I take off, "But it's restricted; for employees only."

I'm already at the back door going down the stairs. I dart through traffic and cross the street, looking for his car the whole time. I look up at all the floors of the parking garage and get ready to plan my attack. I start at ground level and search for any car sitting in a parking space with their lights on. I debate whether to run up each ramp floor by floor but decide the stairs are quicker. I snatch the door to the stairwell and the door knob bangs against the brick wall. I jolt up the stairs by three's and make it to the next floor in seconds. I step one foot outside of the stairwell and listen for any moving vehicles while I again look on both sides of the garage for lights. I do this for two more flights until I see a car that matches the description backing out of the third space on the far-left wall. I sprint to get a closer look. It's him. I wave my free hand as I run and block his path. I slam my arm and half my body on the side of his hood, out of sheer exhaustion.

"Wait! Please!"

He rolls his window down, "Pastor Darnell? What are you thinking!"

I nod my head emphatically as I feel my lungs up with air.

"I just got off the phone. I just received the last vote."

"But wait." I say in almost a whisper still trying to catch my breath. "This is what I wanted to show you." I take the papers out of the folder and offer them.

He looks me up and down. "I wish you would have shown this much passion yesterday." He takes the papers and examines them, then reads. He looks up at me and reads again. "Well, this changes everything. Forget about the vote. I hereby proclaim you to still be the pastor of Abiding Grace Church."

I close my eyes and let out a big sigh.

"Congratulations, Pastor, well done."

# 41 Nicole

I'M PRAISING GOD from the time the man says, 'this changes everything.' As soon as I get back to my car, I call Darnell, but I get no answer. But he'll find out soon enough. I sit in silence for a long time, thinking about the events that led up to this. My eyes are now so clouded with my own tears that I need to blink in order to see. That blink causes tears to race down my cheeks. I get back to Darnell's home elated. I place the folder on top of his desk and go sit in the living room. I'm so relieved and grateful for God's favor today. Darnell is a wonderful pastor who has the heart for God's people, and I'm overjoyed he gets to keep his position. Our church needs him. I may not agree with everything he does or some of the decisions he's made but I know he has the right motives and I know he makes every effort possible to seek God's face and hear from Him. He may get it wrong sometimes, but pastors aren't perfect. Darnell is as human as the rest of us, but he does have a special calling to lead God's people and I believe being a shepherd is the hardest but probably the most fulfilling job there is.

I'll be careful to pick my battles from now on. I'll give him the benefit of the doubt, after all, he consults with other pastors and I'm sure he knows things I don't know, since he's the one who goes to the pastoral conferences and takes special classes. He's exposed to much more than I. Some of our issues are mere opinion anyway and based on our own unique frame of reference. The most important thing is that he's hearing from God (he definitely spends more time in his presence than I do), preaching the word of God, while rightly dividing it with truth and conviction; and he's living a Godly lifestyle. *Lord, did it take all this for me to realize that? Surely there was another way.*

I lean back and close my eyes. I think back over the past few weeks. Nothing could have prepared me for the events that have taken place. I'm at peace even though I don't have a job, or a man. I know that all things work together for good to them that love God, to those that are called according to his purpose. My life is in His hands and I know he'll work it all out in the end. It might not be pretty but as long as it has purpose, I'm satisfied. I smile to myself but I'm also smiling inwardly to my Father, out of amazement knowing that he knows what's best and wants the best for me.

I am overcome with immense joy and an intense heat comes over me. I can feel it come from my belly to my chest. I can sense light shining on my face and I'm almost scared to open my eyes. Could I be so blessed to have a visitation of an angel? My chest starts to pound as I brace myself to open my eyes.

And it's, it's—

Just my laptop. The screen on my laptop is so bright. Wait! It's my laptop! It's *my* laptop! I look down at *my* body and can't help but feel myself all over, despite the sweats. I'm screaming. I jump up from the couch and go to the nearest mirror. I'm looking at myself like I've just found my long-lost twin. I touch my face so gently as though I'm afraid it may break. I shred the sweat top, so I can get a closer look at my body, I just want to see it. My girls are back, nicely tucked into my bra and I can't help but grab them.

I start crying as I stare at my reflection. I turn around and look at my condo. *Thank you, Jesus. Thank you, Jesus.* I fall to my knees in uncontrollable sobs.

\*\*\*

I go back to the couch to look at my laptop and see what Darnell has been working on. He was genuinely looking for me another job. I look at the notepad and see lists of positions with contact information beside it. I turn page after page and the front and back of three pages are all filled with line after line of job information. I start to tear up again at how thoughtful this man is.

# 42 Darnell

I'M TRYING MY best to make things right with Nicole. I know I lost her job but I'm doing all I can to make sure she gets another one, hopefully even better. I should probably be doing this same thing for myself because I don't even remember if I get a severance package from the pastorate or not. If I do, I know it won't last long.

I just finished showering. I think better when I'm surrounded by any kind of water and I needed to clear my head after looking at the clock and knowing the time had passed for the committee to make a decision about me. I'm sure Nicole just didn't have it in her to tell me the bad news. Now I'm back vigorously searching for possible positions Nicole would like. I set the pen down for a minute and lean back, pinching the bridge of my nose. I need a short break.

I think about the preceding weeks and how having another perspective is vital in ministry, especially when it's one that disagrees with you. There's nothing wrong with opposite opinions; in fact, it's quite healthy no matter who it comes from. Our church is diverse, and I need to make sure my leadership and ministers reflect that same diversity, so we can meet the needs of everyone in our congregation and beyond the four walls of the church.

I've learned a lot about Nicole as a person and as a member of my church. She's more than just a member, she's a worker in the vineyard and she's very dedicated and effective at everything she does. She wears a lot of hats at the church on top of her demanding career. She's very skilled, talented, and sharp. I need to really listen to what she has to say, she has been supporting this ministry long before I arrived, and I can benefit from her unique insight of being so close to her previous pastor. I'll remember to take her direct answers as a sign of passion and conviction for what she believes in, not that she's trying to be rude or challenge my authority.

*Lord, what am I doing? I'm talking like I'm still the pastor, but I'm sure they let me go.* Maybe this is just not for me. They warned us about this in seminary. Most pastors don't make it past five years, most of no fault of their own since some so-called Christians can act worse than the world. I shake my head at the thought. No pastor really has job security, but I know I can always go back to sales and get a job anywhere.

I feel heat in my chest. It can't be heartburn, I haven't eaten anything. It feels good though, like a ball of sunshine is permeating through me, almost like how I feel when I'm on my second wind after a workout. I open my eyes and I, I'm in my house? I glance at my body and I'm me again! *Lord, I thank you.* My hand immediately goes south. I check to make sure my package is intact and let out a huge sigh of relief. *Thank you, Jesus.* I fall flat on my face and pray.

***

I get up to call Nicole. I find my phone. She picks up immediately.

"I'm me!"

I laugh. "And I'm me."

"I see your list here. Thank you for trying to get me employed again."

"It's the least I can do. Hey, maybe we can go file for unemployment together."

"Well, I think it's called fraud if you file when you already have a job."

"What do you mean?"

"You're still my pastor. You got your job back."

"You mean they voted to keep me? Wow, after my dismal showing yesterday, I didn't know what would happen."

"Actually, it was because of something else. I mean they could have still come to the same conclusion, but I was able to convince Minister Thaddeus with something else."

"But how?"

"I was looking through your filing cabinet, I just didn't know what for, and I found the contract you signed at your first church."

"OK?"

"Are you looking at it?"

"I'm headed there now." I see the folder on the top of my desk and when I open it, the contract is the first thing I see. "OK. I've got it."

"Look in the middle, in the section where you had to initial, it's about two or three bullets down where it reads something like '*I understand I will be granted the appointment of pastor only after a successful three-month probationary period.*'"

"Which the other letter shows was revoked before the time was up, so I never did officially obtain the pastoral role. Huh. Why didn't I think of that? Thank you, Nicole. I'm grateful, I can't thank you enough."

She relays a soft 'you're welcome' and we discuss what we need to do next.

# 43 Nicole

DARNELL STANDS AT the podium, his eyes pleading with me not to do or say anything that would embarrass him any more than I already have. My eyelids and my head, nod in response, saying without words, *you can trust me.* He braces the congregation. "Before I give the sermon this morning, Sister Freeman would like to share a few words with us. She didn't share with me what she's going to talk about, so we'll all be surprised together." He turns and looks me in the eyes, slightly shakes his head, and chuckles. "But I don't think surprises can really bother me as much as they used to." I can't help but answer with a shy smile and I give a knowing shrug. "Please welcome our very own, Ms. Nicole Freeman."

I know people are clapping, because I see hands touching in slow motion, but their sound is too faint, like a low lull surrounded by the intense drum beat of my pounding heart. I brace myself at the podium and begin.

"Good morning."

"Good morning," the congregation answers in unison.

"I've learned so much these past few weeks, more than I ever thought I wanted, yet, still probably not enough of what I need to, but I have learned. I've learned a lot about myself, but even more about my pastor, our pastor. And that's what I want to share with you this morning."

"OK Sister, go ahead."

"Alright teach us," the encouragement rolls in from around the sanctuary.

"Pastors have the hardest job of all. It's the most envied, most misunderstood, most judged, most sought after for those who aren't even qualified, and many times the most avoided for those who are the most qualified, spiritually and professionally, because of the fickle people they have the task to serve. And I'm not just talking about you, I'm talking about me too. It goes beyond an average person's nine to five job, where we punch in and punch out and take as many breaks as we can in between." A few chuckles sprinkle through the crowd.

"This man gets up at five every morning, but instead of punching a clock, he punches the floor, with his knees. Before most of us have done our last rollover in bed, he's already spent hours talking to The Father on our behalf. He spends countless hours studying The Word so that he can teach us and govern his own life. He holds himself to the highest standards and denies himself things that he has every right to enjoy, just so he won't be a stumbling block to any of us. And if we're honest, we hold him to a higher standard than we do our own selves. I'll be the first to admit, I didn't appreciate him like I should have, but that stops now."

I turn to Darnell. "I've already asked God to forgive me but I'm apologizing now in front of everyone here for the times I've misjudged you, was critical, negative, murmured… You know we're not that different than the children of Israel who were never satisfied and were a constant drain on Moses. But Pastor, I pray you don't miss your Promise Land, dealing with us. There are some pastors who don't deserve this office, who do give the church a bad name, and even though they are few and far in-between, when they are exposed, all the attention in the media makes it seem like many pastors are bad, but pastors have been demonized long enough. We have a great pastor. And this isn't the first great pastor our church has had. Pastor Andrews would be proud.

"OK, OK," a short man shakes his head as he looks around for others who agree.

"Say that, Sister" someone yells.

"Those on the outside see it as a job but those who are called consider it a privilege, the privilege of pastoring. Let me shed some light on our pastor. I've been on assignment for the past few weeks, shadowing him," I can't help but smile, "trying to see us through his eyes. And boy, I tell you, if it were me, I would've quit a long time ago. But I'm not called to be the shepherd of this flock, he is."

When I look over to verbally say thank you in front of hundreds of witnesses, to vocalize what each one of us parishioners should be thinking, I stop short. I can only get out "Pastor, I thank—" because I'm stunned. He's chewing on his lips, his best attempt to not come totally unglued. He had let the tears flow long ago. I see multiple streaks that have raced down his face which he keeps wiping away with a handkerchief right before they break free from his chin and fall to the floor. I'm paralyzed for a few seconds but regain myself. I quickly turn back to the podium and center my body toward the congregation, although by now I can't see anyone from the moisture that has clouded my vision and threatens to burst through like rain. "I thank you, Pastor. We thank you. And we truly appreciate all that you do." I'm saved by the thunderous applause, which also shakes loose not only my tears, but my regret and shame, and revives my gratefulness for this amazing man I get the privilege to call Pastor.

# 44 Darnell

THIS IS THE first time I'm back in my own body and standing behind the pulpit. I address the congregation. "I'm so grateful to be standing in front of you all this morning. First, I need to apologize to all of you who expect more from your pastor. Yes, that was me, Yes, I did it. Yes, it was wrong. I'm sure you may be wondering why I did it, so to expel any rumors, I'll just say it. I was defending the honor of a woman and I didn't think. Pastors have feelings to, but there's no excuse for how I reacted and I'm asking you to forgive me for what I did and for any attention that was placed on our church because of it. I deeply regret it and I hope you accept my sincere apology, so we can move on from here."

"Well, over the past few weeks, and thank God it was only a few," I murmur under my breath, as I catch Nicole giggling, "I've sure learned a lot about myself, and in some ways through the eyes of you. It's as if the Lord allowed me to feel what you feel, to see things from your perspective. And I want to make some changes based on what the Lord has shown me. It's been brought to my attention that we go out too much, that I accept too many invitations to other church events. I understand you have jobs and have to get up the next morning to go to work. And no, I don't go to all these invitations because I'm lonely and don't have a life." I say this as I look straight at Sis. Geneva. And if I can read minds, she's saying *Oh Lord, you didn't have to show him that!* She quickly breaks eye contact.

Even though I don't go to a secular job, I do get up at 5am every morning and check in with the master. He lays you on my heart and I pray, and I labor in this word because I want to be a pastor you can be proud of, that He can talk to and through."

"Amen! Go 'head," shouted the congregation.

"As hard as some of you work on your paying jobs, then you come to the church and put in more time...your dedication and loyalty is much appreciated, and I think I may have taken that for granted. I'm sorry. Rest assured God sees. And His reward is far greater than any you can get from man. But when you know better, you do better. I don't know if I'm able to do this with many roles, but I will look at giving some sort of salary to different positions in our church that require a great deal of time commitment, one being my secretary. I call Sis. Nicole almost every day for one thing or another. And I didn't realize how much of a strain that can be. She's got her own job, a stressful job that takes up a lot of time, as I've come to realize. And I don't want to be a burden." Nicole meets my gaze and smiles. "Maybe the praise and worship leader is another position we can start compensating, I don't know. I realize it may seem like I'm giving preferential treatment to some jobs over others, but there are some positions that require skill, like the musician and the—"

"It takes skill to teach these kids too, Pastor," Sis Florence shouts from the back.

"I know Sister, I know. I don't have all the answers, this is new to me but one thing I can say, is that I have some wise counselors who I'm sure will steer me in the right direction. And of course, I'll always listen to what you the members have to say. I'm not perfect, but I'm your pastor."

# 45 Darnell

I'M SO OVERJOYED to be myself again, so I open the church up every night this week for anyone to come in and talk to me about anything they'd like to see done differently with the church or the various ministries we have. There are no appointments, just walk-ins. Although I probably should have one of my deacons or another minister here, it's just me and Nicole. Nicole greets them as they come in, then she and I compare any mental notes we have from our encounters with them during the days of our switch up, so I can get up to speed and avoid glossing over anything important.

This day, I get off of a call with my own pastor and am a few minutes late starting the open sessions. I start towards the kitchen to get a quick snack to bring back to my office, which I intend to eat between sessions. I turn the corner and see Nicole is writing something down, then my body transitions into slow motion. I see them. The two women I encountered outside the church while in Nicole's body. They are walking toward the table and Nicole stands to greet them. She sees me out of the corner of her eye and turns to ask if I need something. With her back turned to the ladies, I see them wince. Before I can answer Nicole, the lady who had been wearing the hat that day speaks up.

"Uh, Darnell, may I speak with you for a minute?"

"That's Pastor Darnell. Please put a handle on it, Ma'am." I say.

She blinks and takes a half step back. I still remember their seething schemes. Nicole has no idea about my altercation with them while I was in her body, but I've got to nip this in the bud. I'm about to see if they are really here for the right reasons.

"Thank you for coming." I tell them while I reach down and kiss Nicole on the cheek. She flinches and looks up at me, so I pull her close and whisper in her ear, "I'll explain later, just follow my lead."

I turn back to the lady and her watchdog; both of their mouths are wide open. It takes all that's within me not to burst out laughing. "Nicole will take care of you while I go get something from the kitchen." And for good measure, I glance back to Nicole and say, "I'll be right back, baby." She has a blank stare, so I squeeze her hand, the most inconspicuous hint I can give, and she got it.

"OK, Love," she shoots back. Clever. Perfect. The picture of those two biddies, their mouths still frozen, puts a spark in my walk.

I get back to the sanctuary only to find Nicole.

"Where are those two ladies?" I ask.

She looks at me "I don't know what just happened. One of them said I was slick and the other rolled her eyes at me."

I explain the whole situation and what *she* said to them several days before and we have a good laugh. They'll probably never set foot in this church again, but I do hope they have a change of heart. I'm still praying for them to be saved if they're not, and to be delivered.

# 46 Nicole

I WOKE UP this morning earlier than I ever have being me, not as early as I naturally woke up in pastor's body, but still impressive for my standards. I'm lying in bed thinking about what I'm going to do. I don't want to look for another job, but I must. I'll file for unemployment and take a couple weeks off before I look for something else. I now understand why the Lord allowed us to swap bodies. I've learned so much in the past weeks, of what he goes through on a regular basis being a pastor, although I'm sure what I experienced was just a smidgen of the problems he's called to handle. But I guess I learned everything too late. If I would have learned sooner, I'd still have my job. Well, where one door closes, He can allow another one to open. I know all things happen for a reason. After I pray, I'll pack up the company's property and proceed to the office. I swoop the covers back and get on my knees.

Heavenly Father, you are holy, righteous and mighty. You are an amazing loving father. You have all power. Forgive me for any sins I've committed, whether knowingly or unknowingly, anything I've said or done that was against your will, any evil thoughts that I let linger. I confess them to you and I thank you for casting my sins in the sea of forgetfulness, never to rise against me. I submit myself to you, my will, my emotions, my desires; I totally surrender to your will and plans for my life. Lord, I thank you, not for allowing me to go through this test, but for bringing me out. You are a faithful God and I ask that you restore to me my job. Somehow, someway, give me my job back. You know how much work I've put into this and how much it means to me. Even now, as I'm about to turn in my things, I still know that nothing is too hard for you and you are able. And I'm believing you will do it. In Jesus' name, Amen.

\*\*\*

I pull into the parking lot and sit in the car for a while. I look around at the scenery. All the colors look drab, particularly because the sky is gray, not even blue but a dull gray, not a sunbeam in the sky. I feel like I'm in a black and white movie when I should be in high definition. But the weather fits the way I feel. I lean to the passenger seat to pick up the company's assets when my phone rings. I look at the number and take a deep breath. Not sure whether I

237

want to talk to him or not, maybe after I get finished with this. *Oh, why not.* I pick up.

"Nicole?"

"Yes, Darnell."

"I just want you to know again, how sorry I am that I lost your job."

"It's OK. You didn't do it on purpose. You did your best. At least you didn't do something stupid like I did and ruin your reputation."

"Well, I don't blame you. In the heat of the moment, I can understand. Hey…at least you didn't get beat up. Maybe people will think twice when they come up to me any kind of way. You heard what the news reporter called me—"

"The Punching Pastor," we both say. We get a good laugh out of that.

"Have you left the job yet?"

"No," I say with a sigh. "I'm about to go in now."

"OK. Just remember, everything happens for a reason. You're His child and he'll take care of you no matter what."

"I know, I know."

We hang up and I look at the entrance of the building. *Might as well get this over with.* I grab my stuff and march inside.

I go straight to the Human Resources department and hope no one from my own department sees me. I already feel humiliated, I don't need any side glances or sympathy. I'm told the woman who called me has stepped away from her desk, but I can go ahead and have a seat in her office. I set the box containing their laptop, docking station, and charging cords on her desk. Then I remember to take the security card and badge out of my purse and place it right on top of her desk, so she won't ask me for it. They may or may not have already decommissioned it, I didn't have the heart to try it at the front entrance, I just waited for someone else to open the door and walked in right behind them. I know how this works. I've seen too many people get fired or quit and some have their credentials revoked before they even leave the parking lot. At least my boss gave me the benefit of the doubt and let me, well Darnell, bring my laptop home. I was able to take all my personal stuff off of it. Actually, I'm not sure if Gary meant to do it, or was so preoccupied with smoothing things over with the client over dinner that he forgot. I wish Darnell would have retrieved my things from my office but I'm sure they'll bring them down to me. It's fine, I really don't want to go back up there and see my name has already been taken off my door. That would be a slap in the face. You give your blood, sweat, and tears to a company for years and when they get rid of you, they just scrape your name off like you never existed and pop someone else in your place.

I look at my watch and realize I've been sitting here for over twenty minutes. Now I'm getting annoyed. I don't want to do the exit interview anyway, but I have to be pleasant, so they won't mess up my check or contest my unemployment benefits. I start messing with my phone when I hear my boss's voice.

"Nicole, I'm sorry I had to—"

"It's OK," I cut him off. I don't want to hear his drawn-out explanation. *Just let me fill out this paperwork so I can be on my way.* "You did what you had to do. I understand."

"Well that's just it. They still want you as their rep."

"What did you say?"

"Fortunately, I was able to talk to the client over dinner that night. I told them that was not you at all. And they could see by your strong fact-based presentation that you thoroughly did your homework, and you really do know what you're talking about. You just had a bad day, a horrible presentation day and with one of our biggest potential clients, I will add. Now *that*, I couldn't explain. Can you?"

I don't know what to say, I didn't expect to even have a conversation with him, let alone get to keep my job. When the lady from human resources called me this morning to tell me to come in and bring my laptop, that meant I was no longer an employee. *Jesus, help me tell this man something believable.*

"By the way they say they were being so hard on you because they wanted to prepare you for what it would be like to work with the upper management of their firm. They know how brutal they can be, especially to women, so they wanted to get you ready, even if it was by shock treatment. When they first asked me who I recommend working with them and why, I told them you because you're like a bulldog. You don't take any mess and you can hold your own even when others with more titles try to intimidate you."

I scrunch my forehead.

"Yeah, I know. You didn't show it in the meeting with them, but they did their homework too and called around to some of the clients you've worked with in the past and they all gave their stamp of approval. Nicole, all of them had only high remarks. Your hard work payed off...but how can you assure me that misstep won't happen again?"

*Bingo. Thank you, Jesus.* "Sorry sir, I started taking a new medication and I believe it's too strong for me."

"Too strong? From what I saw in there, you may want to get rid of it altogether."

"I'll make sure to tell my doctor to switch it to something else."

"Let me guess, you've been on it for a few weeks."

"Yes, but I stopped taking it myself yesterday, I wasn't going to wait. How did you know?"

"Hmmm, that explains a lot. You definitely need to tell your doctor that it totally changed you; made you forgetful, and I'm sure it messed with your estrogen, or gave you more testosterone or something."

He shakes his head like he's trying to shake out a bad memory, but all I'm thinking is *what did Darnell do?*

"Anyway, I'm glad to have you back. I can see a difference already." He lowers his head to the side and gives me a quick once over. "Weird." He shakes it off and turns to leave. He walks about two steps

down the hall and I hear him say under his breath,
"I'm getting too old for this."

# 47 Darnell

IT'S BEEN A couple of weeks already since Nicole and I have returned to our bodies and we've talked in person every single day. I look forward to each moment I spend with her, even if we're talking about church matters.

"You're smiling from ear to ear. What gives?" I ask.

"You know that client of mine that you almost lost my job with?"

"I'll never forget."

"They have expanded my role and given me responsibility over their other four locations as well."

"Congratulations."

"Thank you. This means a nice bonus and another increase in pay."

"Well deserved My Lady. So now you really forgive me."

She shakes her head. "Darnell, I told you I had forgiven you the first time. And I really meant it, no matter what would have happened. You truly forgave me right, even though people probably won't look at you quite the same?"

"Of course, And I don't worry about people. I let God handle it. And if somebody's going to throw me away for one act of indiscretion, they need to get their own courtroom. God doesn't even judge like that and he's the only one who's qualified to do so."

A soft breeze billows a few strands of her hair and I can't help myself. I move my hand along her forehead and gently pull her hair behind her ear. Her eyes invite me in.

"May I kiss you?" I ask.

"I don't think this is going to work."

I pull her closer. "Who else is ever going to be able to top this? We have something very unique. And we can't tell anyone about what we've been through; who would believe it?" I display a big grin. "No one can ever come any closer than we have. I've seen you and I like what I see." Her face turns stone white. "No, not that. I mean you, your insides, what you're all about, your heart," I quickly explain.

"And that didn't turn you off?" Her eyes are skeptical but hopeful.

"No. You're not perfect, but as you've come to find out, neither am I. What do you say? Will you give us a chance?"

She nods, and I lean in. One simple kiss, more than a peck, but our lips only touch once. One lingering kiss that seems to be in slow motion but with all the hope and longing that I could ask for. She grabs my hand and we stare into each other's eyes.

She smiles and says, "One day at a time, Darnell," and looks out into the distance.

I need not reply with words. I simply hold her as she tucks her head in the lock of my shoulder. Weeks being inside my body, she thinks she knows me inside and out but one thing she doesn't know is I'm a man who's willing to wait as long as it takes for her to be mine.

## *The End*

# Book Club Questions

1. What do you think would be the hardest part of living in the body of the opposite sex?
2. What do you think would be the easiest?
3. In what ways do we have a double standard for pastors or hold them to a higher standard?
4. Do you think this is unfair or are we justified in doing so? Explain.
5. Do you think pastors have it easier or harder than others?
6. What do you think your pastor wishes his congregation would understand about him?
7. If you are a pastor, what do you want your congregation to know/understand about you?
8. In what ways can you show appreciation to and for your pastor? Explain. (Note that these are two different things.)
9. In what ways do you think the church is changing/or adjusting with the times? Discuss the good and/or bad effects of these changes.
10. In what areas should churches remain the same?
11. Why do you think less people attend church? Is it just the way of the world, meaning the Bible is just fulfilling itself, or has the church become ineffective?
12. Is it true that fornication is seen as an accepted sin among single believers?

13. Should people in church leadership be held to a higher standard?

14. If so, how would this be monitored in practical terms?

15. What positions in the church should be paid? And why? Or should we all be unpaid volunteers because whatever our gifts, skills, or talents, they are being used in God's service?

# Note from the Author

I hope you have enjoyed this silly book. Yes, we know this could never happen, but the point is for each of us to try and step into the other's shoes for a moment and ponder what our pastor has to go through every day, and for pastors not to lose sight of what members must endure as well. I tried to shed light on that, although I just scratched the surface. I hope you will continue the conversation with your fellow parishioners <u>and</u> your pastor. We're all in this together.

Thank you for going on this journey with me.

**Please show your support by leaving a review for this book, wherever you purchased it <u>and</u> on Goodreads.com.** It helps me reach new readers.

If you would like me to come speak at your event or attend your book club meeting I can be reached at:

**Email:** Info@ShalondaMcFarland.com

**Facebook:** Shalonda McFarland Ministry

**Website:** ShalondaMcFarland.com

# About the Author

**SHALONDA MCFARLAND** is an author, speaker, and Gospel recording artist. She enjoys writing unique fiction, and non-fiction Christian-centered books. Wise Witness Ministry, which Shalonda birthed out of her book and workbook *A Christian's Worst Witness…From Being Broke To Being Blessed* is focused on teaching Christians how to handle money God's way. Her articles on Christian finance have been featured in various church mediums and Christian publications, including magazines and journals.

Mrs. McFarland is a dynamic, heart-felt, action-provoking speaker, who delivers a biblically-based message diverse with everyday examples and strives to live out her personal brand of *serving by adding value and exceeding expectations.*

Shalonda and her husband Doug have five children, Rakaya, Doug Jr., Mariah, Jordan, and Melanie, and reside in the Houston, Texas area.